"You're tense," Stone said.

His fingers gently stroked her shoulders, kneading her muscles at the exact spot where they knotted. He'd always known just where and how to touch her, how to make her relax, how to make her melt.

Jamie knew she should move away or at least tell him to stop, but she was strangely rooted to the chair, unable to move. His fingers worked their way up her neck and she rolled her head forward. It felt like pure heaven. Surely a few moments wouldn't hurt.

She closed her eyes and inhaled his clean, soapy scent, a scent she recognized as his shaving cream. It stirred up memories...of Stone lathering his face, wearing only a towel around his waist; of sharing the bathroom mirror with him on hurried mornings; of a playful shaving-cream fight that had ended with a heated lovemaking session in the shower....

Their marriage had lasted only a year, but the memories would last a lifetime.

D0775770

Dear Reader,

In 1993 beloved, bestselling author Diana Palmer launched the FABULOUS FATHERS series with *Emmett* (SR#910), which was her 50th Silhouette book. Readers fell in love with that Long, Tall Texan who discovered the meaning of love and fatherhood, and ever since, the FABULOUS FATHERS series has been a favorite. And now, to celebrate the publication of the *50th* FABULOUS FATHERS book, Silhouette Romance is very proud to present a brand-new novel by Diana Palmer, *Mystery Man,* and Fabulous Father Canton Rourke.

Silhouette Romance is just chock-full of special books this month! We've got *Miss Maxwell Becomes a Mom,* book one of Donna Clayton's new miniseries, THE SINGLE DADDY CLUB. And Alice Sharpe's *Missing: One Bride* is book one of our SURPRISE BRIDES trio, three irresistible books by three wonderful authors about very unusual wedding situations.

Rounding out the month is Jodi O'Donnell's newest title, *Real Marriage Material,* in which a sexy man of the land gets tamed. Robin Wells's *Husband and Wife...Again* tells the tale of a divorced couple reuniting in a delightful way. And finally, in *Daddy for Hire* by Joey Light, a hunk of a man becomes the most muscular nanny there ever was, all for love of his little girl.

Enjoy Diana Palmer's *Mystery Man* and all of our wonderful books this month. There's just no better way to start off springtime than with six books bursting with love!

Regards,

Melissa Senate
Senior Editor
Silhouette Books

Please address questions and book requests to:
Silhouette Reader Service
U.S.: 3010 Walden Ave., P.O. Box 1325, Buffalo, NY 14269
Canadian: P.O. Box 609, Fort Erie, Ont. L2A 5X3

HUSBAND AND WIFE...AGAIN

Robin Wells

Silhouette

R O M A N C E™

Published by Silhouette Books

America's Publisher of Contemporary Romance

To Ken, my forever love.

With special thanks to speech pathologist Nancy Reed
for sharing her knowledge with me.

 SILHOUETTE BOOKS

ISBN 0-373-19214-2

HUSBAND AND WIFE...AGAIN

Copyright © 1997 by Robin Rouse Wells

This edition published by arrangement with Harlequin Books S.A.

Printed in U.S.A.

Books by Robin Wells

Silhouette Romance

The Wedding Kiss #1185
Husband and Wife...Again #1214

ROBIN WELLS

Before becoming a full-time writer, Robin was a public relations executive whose career ran the gamut from writing to producing award-winning videos to organizing pie-throwing classes taught by circus clowns. At other times in her life she has been a model, a reporter and even a charm school teacher. But her lifelong dream was to become an author, a dream no doubt inspired by having parents who were both librarians, and who passed on their love of books.

Robin lives just outside New Orleans with her husband and two young daughters, Taylor and Arden. Although New Orleans is known as America's Most Romantic City, Robin says her personal romantic inspiration is her husband, Ken.

Robin is an active member of the Southern Louisiana chapter of the Romance Writers of America. She won the national association's 1995 Golden Heart Award for Best Short Contemporary Novel and was a finalist in the 1994 "Heart of the Rockies" RWA contest.

When she's not writing, Robin enjoys gardening, antiquing, discovering new restaurants and spending time with her family.

Stone's recipe for
SEDUCTION CHICKEN

(Serves two)

2 skinned chicken breasts
Salt
Pepper
Chili powder
Jar of Mexican salsa
1 ripe avocado, peeled and sliced
Sliced aged Swiss cheese

Place chicken breasts in greased cooking dish. Sprinkle lightly with salt, pepper and a pinch of chili powder, then top each breast with about a tablespoon of salsa. Bake at 375° F for 45 minutes or until done. Cover chicken with avocado slices. Drizzle more salsa over the avocado, then cover with sliced cheese. Return to oven until cheese melts (approximately 5-10 minutes).

Serve to the one you love. If it doesn't heat things up, try a warm embrace—or a hotter salsa!

Chapter One

"What do you mean, we don't have an anchor?" Harold Walker gawked at Jamie over his large studio camera, his grizzled brow wrinkling like an unironed cotton shirt. He jabbed a stubby finger toward the clock on the wall of the darkened television studio. "It's nineteen minutes until airtime! Where the hell is Todd?"

Jamie fought back a rising tide of panic as she picked her way through the cables snaking across the floor. "You know how Todd is. He'll probably breeze in at the last moment."

Harold gave a derisive snort. "Yeah, I know how he is. He's probably sleeping off another bender." He glanced again at the clock, and Jamie followed his gaze. The large black hand was creeping ominously closer to six o'clock. "Better face it, kiddo—even Todd has never cut it this close. What are you going to do if he doesn't show up?"

Jamie's pulse tripped like a teletype machine. She'd been asking herself the very same question. As the producer of KZZZ's early morning news, she was responsible for every aspect of the show.

She bit her lower lip worriedly. She should have called

in a replacement anchor at the first sign Todd was going to
be late—but then, he was late *every* morning. And he'd
never actually missed a newscast. Now it looked as if Todd
was going to be a no-show and there was no time to get a
replacement.

*Oh, mercy. Of all the mornings for Todd to pull such a
stunt, why did he have to pick this one?* The consultant
hired by the station's general manager to improve KZZZ's
news ratings had arrived in town last night and was due to
start work that day. Jamie knew the first thing he'd probably do when he woke up this morning was turn his TV to
channel three, and she had intended to make a great first
impression.

She needed to; she wanted to sell him on the idea of
running a weekly series to help hard-to-adopt children find
homes. She'd even sneaked a story about the children into
this morning's news lineup in hopes that if he understood
their plight, he'd be more inclined to go along with the
concept.

But first she had to make sure there *was* a newscast.

What would Stone do in this situation? It was a question
Jamie often asked herself when faced with a dilemma at
work. Her ex-husband was the consummate news professional, never at a loss for the right answer, always sure of
himself, and imagining his response to a problem usually
helped her solve it herself. The only flaw with the technique
was that thinking about Stone created a whole other set of
deeper, more emotional problems.

No time for that now, Jamie told herself sternly.

"Has any talent come in early?" she asked the cameraman. "Any reporters? Maybe someone on the weather
staff?"

Harold shook his grizzled head. "I went down to the
break room for a cup of coffee a few minutes ago, and not
a soul was in sight. It's just you, me, the director and the
engineer."

Just the usual staff. At this hour only a skeleton crew
was on duty. Harold had to run the camera, the director

had to stay in the control room and the engineer had to keep the station on the air.

Her stomach clenched in a nervous knot. A producer who allowed "dead air" to run in her time slot might as well kiss her job goodbye, and Jamie knew how scarce TV jobs were in a small market like Fairfield, Texas.

It was time to make an executive decision. Unfortunately, only one solution came to mind, and the very thought of it made her blood run cold.

She drew a deep, shaky breath and tried to swallow. Her throat felt like a hard-boiled egg had wedged in it sideways. "Well, it looks like I'm reading the news this morning."

The cameraman's eyes bugged beneath their droopy lids. Jamie told herself to ignore his incredulous expression as she dashed toward the dressing room next door, but she couldn't help but wonder if he were more aghast at her lack of experience or her unlikely appearance. In faded blue jeans and an old T-shirt, she knew she hardly looked like anchor material, but that was the least of her worries.

What the cameraman didn't know, and what had her heart pounding so loudly she could hardly hear herself think, was the fact that she was terrified—*petrified*—of public speaking.

No, that wasn't quite right, Jamie thought as she grabbed a brush from the tray of hair care supplies and whisked her shoulder-length blond hair into a low ponytail.

She was petrified of public stuttering.

"You're over it," Jamie muttered to her reflection in the lighted mirror. "You haven't stuttered in years. Just stay calm, think about each story as you read it and you'll be fine."

But the truth was she hadn't tested it in more than a decade. She wrapped a rubber band around her hair and snatched a tube of lipstick from the tray. "You've overcome it," she fiercely whispered to her image. "You're a producer, you've got a show to put on the air—and you can't let those kids down."

The last thought bolstered her, and she clung to it as she

outlined her lips. She'd visited the Fairfield Children's Home when she'd produced a story about children with special needs, and the youngsters she'd met had touched her heart. The home needed a way to publicize the dozens of children waiting for adoption, and she was determined to help.

The lipstick was ruby red, far brighter than she usually used. She started to wipe it off and rummage for another shade, but a glance at her watch changed her mind.

A rack across from the dressing room's small shower held a sparse selection of clothing. Jamie peeled off her shirt and threw on a white blouse with an ascot tie, buttoning it with one hand as she glanced at her watch with the other.

Six minutes until air. Just enough time to dash back to the newsroom, grab the blazer she'd worn against the chill March air and race to the set. "Please, God," she whispered. "Let Todd be here by now!"

She clung to the thought as she pushed open the door to the studio and wasn't aware of how much hope she'd invested in it until she saw the brightly lit, still-empty set. Her feet seemed set in concrete.

Harold gestured frantically. "Come on! We've just got two minutes and I need to get a voice level on you."

Two minutes, and she would be appearing before a quarter million viewers. Jamie made her way into the glaring lights, sat behind the anchor desk and clipped the mike to her lapel with a shaking hand, casting about for reassuring thoughts. At least she knew the material; she'd written the script herself just an hour ago.

"Okay—give me a mike check," Harold said.

"One, two, three." Even to her ears, her voice sounded weak and hesitant. She cleared her throat and tried again. "One, two, three."

Harold nodded in satisfaction. "Got it."

"One minute," boomed a voice over the intercom.

Jamie jumped. Even though the director called the one-minute warning from the glass-enclosed control booth above the studio in the same fashion before each newscast, it sounded like the voice of doom this morning.

"Are you okay?" Harold asked. "You look kinda pale."

Jamie merely nodded, not trusting herself to speak. The lights were so hot she could smell scorching dust motes, yet a shiver ran up her neck.

"There's a glass of water under the desk," Harold said gently.

Jamie gave him a grateful smile and took a swallow, but the water somehow slid down her throat without managing to wet her mouth. Her heart was pounding so loudly she was afraid the mike would pick it up.

What was it her speech therapist had told her as a teenager? "Concentrate on what you're trying to communicate and don't worry about how you sound." The key to overcoming her stuttering had been to become so absorbed in *what* she was doing that she couldn't think about *how* she was doing it. Jamie had honed her concentration skills to such a laser-sharp level that her grandmother used to accuse her of going into a trance.

"Thirty seconds," boomed the director.

Jamie gathered up the sheaf of papers in front of her and stared at the first story, trying to summon up that trancelike concentration now.

The words seemed to swim on the page like letters in a bowl of alphabet soup. Panic tightened her throat. Oh, mercy. She was too nervous to even make sense of the story, much less read it aloud!

The strains of the opening music to the newscast filled the studio. Terrified, Jamie gazed at the TV monitor to the left of the set and watched the show's introduction. "And now..." intoned the recording of the silken-voiced announcer, "it's time for the morning news with Todd Dodson."

She tried to move her head, but it seemed to have turned to granite. She was literally paralyzed with fright, as helpless as a frog in a flashlight beam. She couldn't even breathe. If she didn't do something fast, she was going to pass out!

A relaxation technique her ex-husband had once mentioned flashed through her mind and she grabbed at it like a life preserver: *picture someone in their underwear.*

The only person in her line of vision was Harold. He was the boxer-short type, no question about it, and he probably wore garters with his socks. The thought of the lumpy man standing in the studio, naked except for knee highs and a pair of baggy drawers pulled high on his bulbous belly, helped her draw a shaky breath. Concentrating on the comical image, she even managed a smile.

The red light blinked on the camera and Harold's arm came down in a gesture like a flagman at an auto race.

Jamie looked directly at the camera, straining not to squint against the glaring lights. "Good morning. I'm Jamie Erickson, and I'm filling in for Todd Dodson."

When the red light blinked off thirty minutes later, Jamie drew a ragged breath and slumped forward in the chair.

"That was great, doll!" Harold called.

Great? Flat-out awful would be more like it. She had focused so intently on the content of the stories that she'd completely ignored her delivery, and she was sure she'd sounded like the rankest of rank amateurs. Her eyes had filled with tears when she read the story about children awaiting adoption, her voice had cracked when she read about the plight of a homeless family, and if she'd sounded half as outraged as she'd felt when she read the government waste story, she had probably come across as a raving lunatic.

Not exactly appropriate news anchor demeanor. The general manager would have a cow. She could only pray that the consultant was a late sleeper.

Jamie mustered a feeble grin. "Thanks for your help, Harold." The image of the ungainly man in his boxers again flitted through her mind, and her smile gained momentum. Harold would never know just how much help he'd actually been.

"Thanks, guys," she called to the engineer and director as they left the control booth. Harold clamped a lens cap on the camera then glanced up at the clock. "It's break time. Want to grab some breakfast?"

Jamie shook her head. "No, thanks. I'm too keyed up to eat. I think I'll just stay here and decompress." She ran a finger around the high neck of the borrowed blouse, feeling like she'd just finished a marathon. "As a matter of fact, I think I'll try out that shower in the dressing room."

Harold flipped off the spotlights as he left the studio, the heavy door silently closing behind him. The set was suddenly dark and quiet. Jamie drew in a deep breath, finally able to collect her thoughts.

She'd done it. She might not have been great, but she'd put the show on the air and she hadn't stuttered. The tension in her stomach began to uncoil as she rose from the chair, a sense of amazement giving way to satisfaction.

She'd actually done it. A burst of pride pulsed through her as she made her way out of the studio and down the corridor. She'd faced her own personal demon and won, and by golly, it felt good. As a matter of fact, it felt great.

The thought put a bounce in her step, and when the dressing room door closed behind her, she broke into dance. "Yes!" she yelled, pumping her arm victoriously in the air and flinging her jacket over the makeup mirror. She quickly unbuttoned the borrowed blouse, ripped it off and twirled it overhead, running in place like a quarterback who'd just scored a touchdown.

She added a few bumps and grinds for good measure, then reached back to unfasten her bra as she burst into song. "I am woman..."

"And quite a woman at that."

Jamie froze. Someone was in the dressing room with her—someone whose voice was deep and masculine and eerily familiar.

It couldn't be. She spun around, her heart in her throat,

to find a tall, broad-shouldered man standing in the shadows in the corner of the room, an amused smile etched on his rugged face.

It was a face she knew all too well, even though she hadn't seen it in three years. A face that still flitted through her dreams at night and, though she'd never admit it to a soul, haunted her waking thoughts all too often.

It was the face of her ex-husband, and it wore a sexy, crooked grin.

Her pulse went into overdrive and it was a long moment before she could think, much less form words. "Stone!" she finally managed. "What are you doing here?"

He flashed a dimple as his smile widened, deepening the laugh lines around his eyes. "I was waiting to talk to you, but right now I'm enjoying the floor show."

Jamie stared at him, trying to absorb the fact of his presence, then clutched at her chest, suddenly aware that she wore no shirt and that her unlatched bra was slipping precariously. He laughed, revealing a row of white, even teeth, and his golden eyes raked her with frank masculine appreciation. "Relax, Jamie. There's nothing you've got I haven't seen before."

The words and his slow, roving gaze sent a rush of heat to her face. Jamie gritted her teeth, determined not to let him know how profoundly he affected her. "There's nothing I've got you'll ever see again." She jerked around, her back toward him, and grabbed her jacket, clutching it to her chest with one hand as she desperately tried to fasten her bra with the other.

"Relax, Jamie," he repeated softly, so close behind her it made her jump. He reached out and fastened her bra for her. "I didn't mean to startle you."

His fingers brushed her skin as he performed the intimate task, and a shiver chased up her spine. She jerked away as soon as he finished. Damn him! After three years of divorce, he had no right to make her heart race and her skin burn and her knees feel as rubbery as Gumby's.

She was in shock, that was all. She was a nervous wreck

from the newscast, and he'd given her a terrible start. The way her pulse was pounding had nothing to do with her feelings for him.

She'd feel better once she was decent. Still clutching the blazer against her chest, she managed to thrust her arms through the armholes. She turned to face him, wearing the jacket backward.

His face registered pure amusement. "I see you've become quite a fashion trailblazer."

Jamie glared at him. "And I see that your manners have taken a turn for the worse. How dare you barge in here and scare me half to death?" She wrapped her arms across her chest and felt the jacket gape open in the back. "What the heck are you doing here, anyway?"

He perched on the corner of the dressing table, the muscles of his thigh bulging against the fabric of his khaki slacks, and gave her a smile that transformed his face from attractive to devastating. That smile had always melted her like butter in summer sunshine, and she was chagrined to discover she wasn't immune to it now.

"I'm here as a consultant," he replied.

All Jamie could do was stare.

"The company wants to put the station on the market, but they've got to raise the ratings in order to get a decent price," Stone explained. "I'm here to find ways to do that."

"But—but I thought you were the news director at a station in Seattle!"

Stone shrugged. "Just a rung on the career ladder. You know how the news industry is."

She knew all too well. The frequent moves had caused major problems in their marriage. "So now you work for a consulting firm?"

"Actually, I formed my own company last year, and it's more than a consulting service. I specialize in hands-on news management."

His own company! But then, she shouldn't really be surprised; he'd always been extremely ambitious. In fact,

Stone's ambition had been the primary reason for their divorce. She'd had no intention of playing second fiddle to his career for the rest of her life. She'd watched her mother play out that scenario with her workaholic father, and she didn't care for it one bit.

Something else he'd said snagged her attention. "What do you mean, 'hands-on management'?"

"I mean I'll be implementing changes, working directly with the staff. Since this station is between news directors, I'll be filling that role."

"For how long?"

"A couple of months. Until the May sweeps period."

Oh, mercy. A couple of months of seeing Stone every day?

He seemed to be reading her mind. "I hope you won't mind working with me, Jamie."

"Why should I mind?" she asked defensively.

He gave her a long, measuring glance. "No reason. No reason at all." He pushed off the vanity table and strode across the room. "I was surprised to learn you were working in news. The last I knew, you were producing documentaries about children's issues for the local PBS station."

Jamie lowered herself onto the dressing table stool. "I was, and I loved it. Unfortunately, the funds dried up."

"So you switched to TV news?"

"Producing jobs are hard to come by in this market."

"You didn't consider looking elsewhere?"

Jamie bristled. The topic of moving had always been a bone of contention between them. Stone had never understood Jamie's longing for a sense of permanence, for roots, for a real home. "No. I'd just bought a house."

His eyebrows flew up in surprise. "Alone?"

"Yes. Why do you ask?"

"I was wondering if your grandmother was living with you."

"Oh." Jamie pretended to study her short, clipped fingernails, unaccountably disappointed that the question wasn't designed to find out if she'd remarried. She was suddenly consumed with curiosity about Stone's own marital status but didn't want him to know she cared enough to ask.

She realized he was still waiting for an answer about her grandmother. "Grams and I are both too independent for that. But my house is just a few blocks from hers."

"How's she doing?"

"Feisty as ever. Still addicted to soap operas, talk shows and sitcoms. When she's not glued to the TV, she's organizing senior citizens tours of Madagascar or Timbuktu."

"Glad to hear it." Stone's lips curved into a smile. "She's quite a gal. I've always thought a lot of her."

Grams had always admired Stone, too, but Jamie would be darned if she'd tell him so.

He loosened his tie and unfastened the top button of his white oxford shirt, his smile lingering on her, and she felt an old, familiar tug in her stomach. She knotted her hands over the spot, unconsciously trying to ward off the pull of attraction.

"You could have knocked me over with a feather this morning when George Milton turned on the TV in his office and I saw you at the anchor desk."

A sick feeling hit Jamie like the Hong Kong flu. "You watched the newscast with the general manager?"

Stone nodded. "Yep. He was as surprised to see you on the air as I was."

"I'll bet." Jamie gnawed her bottom lip. "Look, I can explain. The anchor was a no-show. I know I should have called in a replacement, but I kept thinking he would make it in, and—"

"He agreed with me that you were great."

Jamie stared, unsure she'd heard him correctly. "What?"

Stone gave a single nod. "You were great. Nothing short of genius."

"Stop joking."

"I'm not. You were terrific. You came across as concerned, caring, involved."

Jamie tried to wave her hand dismissively and nearly fell out of her jacket. She carefully pulled it back on her shoulder. "Come on, Stone. An anchor's supposed to be detached and objective."

"Says who?"

The question took her aback. "It's...it's just something everyone knows."

"If the phone calls that came in this morning are any indication, people are sick and tired of getting bad news dished out by a deadpan anchor."

She stared, incredulous. "There were calls?"

Stone nodded. "Dozens of them. They started after the first commercial break and kept on coming. The switchboard was flooded by the time the show was over." He flashed his killer smile. "You've got something, Jamie, and it's *big*. It could carry you to an anchor desk in a major market. Maybe even a network job. You could be a huge success."

Jamie stiffened. "Not everyone shares your definition of success, Stone. It so happens I like producing. Besides, as soon as something opens up, I want to get out of news and back into children's programming."

Stone heaved a sigh. "I was afraid you'd say that." He rubbed his jaw and waited until she met his gaze. "I hate to tell you this, Jamie, but you've just made a career change."

She went perfectly still, unsure she'd heard him correctly. "What do you mean?"

"I mean I've recommended that you be made the new morning and noon anchor."

He had to be kidding. "No way."

He raised his eyebrows. "No way it's possible, or no way you'll do it?"

"Both. Come on, Stone—you know how I feel about public speaking."

"You're still worried about the stuttering?"

Dadblast it! Her stuttering was her own private business. If an old high school chum hadn't happened to mention it once in Stone's presence, he'd never even know she used to have a problem. She'd avoided talking about it when they'd been married, and she sure didn't want him mentioning it at the station now.

When people knew she stuttered, they waited for her to do it, and knowing they were expecting it made her self-conscious, and when she was self-conscious, well, that was when it used to happen.

Dadblast it! Jamie clenched her hands into fists so tightly her fingernails bit into her palms. She needed to convince Stone it wasn't an issue. She straightened her back, thrust out her chin and did her best to appear nonchalant. "Of course not."

She was relieved when he nodded, apparently buying it.

"I didn't think so. I've never heard you stutter in all the time I've known you." He moved behind her, placing his hands on her shoulders. She jumped at the contact.

"You're tense," he said. His fingers gently stroked her shoulders, kneading her muscles at the exact spot where they knotted. He'd always known just where and how to touch her, how to make her relax, how to make her melt.

She knew she should move away or at least tell him to stop, but she was strangely rooted to the chair, unable to move. His touch affected her like a narcotic, making her dazed and dreamy. His fingers worked their way up her neck, and she rolled her head forward. It felt like pure heaven. Surely a few more moments wouldn't hurt.

She closed her eyes and inhaled his clean, soapy scent, a scent she recognized as his shaving cream. It stirred up a storm of steamy memories…of Stone lathering his face, wearing only a towel around his waist; of sharing the bathroom mirror with him on hurried mornings; of a playful shaving cream fight that had ended with a heated lovemaking session in the shower.…

Jamie abruptly opened her eyes to find him watching her in the dressing table mirror. She looked away, rattled and disoriented, and drew a deep breath, striving for a normal tone. "Of course I'm tense. Going on the air made me so nervous I had to imagine the cameraman standing there in his underwear.''

Stone's laughter was as warm and lusty as the memories it evoked. His fingers continued their delicious work. ''The old underwear trick, huh? I'm glad to know I had some influence on your life.''

Oh, he'd had some influence, all right. Their marriage had only lasted a year, but the memories would last a lifetime. Leaning back against the pressure of his hands, a cool breeze drifted up her back where the jacket gaped open behind her. Her mind seemed to open and drift as well. Recollections bombarded her: Stone's hands on her shoulders like this, only he was slipping off the straps of a yellow sundress. Stone's mouth on hers, his lips as soft as suede. Stone's body moving over her, all toned muscles and lean angles and hard, solid man.

A surge of desire, hot and fast and intense, swept through her, leaving her shaken. She'd forgotten how quickly, how thoroughly, he'd always been able to arouse her.

Jamie was suddenly aware that his fingers had worked their way under the jacket. Merciful heavens, what was she doing? She was sitting there daydreaming, falling back under his spell, while Stone threatened to rearrange her entire career!

Alarmed, she jerked away. The stool screeched on the linoleum floor as she abruptly stood and turned to face him. ''Thanks for the back rub. But as for the job recommendation—no thanks.''

''Most people would kill for an opportunity like this, Jamie.''

She straightened, causing the jacket to nearly fall off her shoulder. ''Then I guess I'm not like most people. I'm a behind-the-scenes kind of person, not an in-the-spotlight type. I'm not cut out for it. I'm too shy.''

''Even seasoned anchors are nervous when they go on camera. It's a normal reaction.'' His dimple flashed as he grinned. ''And as for being shy—I remember a few ways you're not shy at all.''

Oh, mercy. The room seemed to grow several degrees warmer. She needed to get the conversation on safer footing—fast. "The station already has an anchor. What about Todd?"

"He committed a fireable offense this morning. If he doesn't lose his job, he'll probably be bumped down to the reporter pool."

Icy fingers of fear tightened around her chest. Stone's jaw was firming into that determined set, the one that meant his mind was made up and a team of oxen couldn't make him budge. If she were going to dissuade him, she had to act fast. "I have some ideas for improving the ratings, Stone, that you should consider before you do something so drastic. There's a children's home filled with kids who're considered unadoptable—kids who don't fit the profile of the cuddly newborn most adopting couples want, kids who are older or disabled. The children are adorable, and I'm certain that if we could show them on TV, we could find homes for them. You said yourself that people are tired of getting bad news from uncaring anchors. Maybe they're just tired of feeling that there's nothing they can do. Maybe if we give them a way to help, they'll tune in."

"Still have a soft spot for children, animals and underdogs, I see," Stone said softly. "That was one of the things I loved about you."

Loved—past tense. Jamie's throat constricted. Well, what did she expect? They were divorced, after all. Besides, if kids and animals were so all-fired important to him, why hadn't he wanted to settle down and have any?

"I think a regular, positive feature would attract viewers," she said doggedly. "You should at least give it a try."

"I've seen similar concepts in other markets," he replied. "They're good community-service tools, but they don't usually have much effect on ratings. Not like putting the right person at the anchor desk."

"Well, I think the folks in our viewing area would tune in to see something positive—especially if we run follow-up stories." The blasted jacket slipped again. She yanked it back in place with one arm, nearly causing it to slide off the other side. "In any case, I'm not the right person for the anchor desk."

He gave her a grin. "Oh, you're the right person, all right. I've never seen anyone generate such a response."

Her grandmother used to say Stone was as persistent as a flea on a dog, and he didn't seem to have lost any of his tenacity. Jamie was running out of angles and starting to panic. "It was a fluke, Stone. It wouldn't happen again. If they make me an anchor, they'll be firing me within a week. Then where will I be?"

"Tell them up front that if it doesn't work out, you want your old job back. Make it a condition of your anchor contract. For that matter, if you're so intent on doing a weekly feature about the kids, make that a condition of your contract, too."

"You're missing the point. I don't want to sign a contract."

"Aren't you already under one?"

"Well, yes."

"If it's the standard contract this station uses, it says you'll provide 'professional services' for a specified time period. If they want those services to be a producer or a news anchor or a janitor, then that's what you've got to do—unless you want to go to the expense of a court fight to try to get out of it."

He wasn't recommending her for the position—he was forcing her to take it. He had her boxed in. Cornered.

And it made her see red. "Let's see if I've got this straight. Thanks to you and your advice, the powers that be want me to work as an anchor, but want to pay me like a lowly producer?"

"No. They want you to sign a new contract." He named a salary figure that made her head reel.

She clenched her jaw stubbornly. Okay, so the money was great. So what? Money wasn't the issue. The issue was that she didn't want to be forced into a position that fit her like shoes on a snake. Unlike Stone, money had never been her principal motivator.

She poured the full force of her wrath into her gaze. "I don't want to do it."

Stone held his palms up. "I'm not the person who's going to make you."

"But you're the consultant. They're acting on your advice. You talked them into it, and you can talk them out of it."

"I can't do that, Jamie. After seeing you on the air this morning, I'm certain you're the ticket to turning this place around. It's my responsibility to tell them the truth."

Stone's unshakable code of ethics was one of the things she'd always admired about him, but that didn't prevent a fresh wave of anger from flooding Jamie's veins. "Who do you think you are to stroll in here and turn my life upside down?"

"I'm the station's consultant, and I'm being paid to give my honest opinion."

"But this is my *life* you're messing with," Jamie protested hotly. "I'll be here long after you've sailed off into the sunset. Just like three years go."

A nerve worked in Stone's jaw. "Wait just a cotton-pickin' minute, Jamie. *You* divorced *me*, remember? I wanted you to move with me to Seattle."

Her fingers tensed into tight fists. "I moved three times in one year for the sake of your almighty career, and I'd just been awarded a grant to produce my first documentary. You didn't consider my feelings enough to even consult me before you accepted a job half a continent away."

Stone's eyes darkened and clouded. "There's no point in rehashing our marriage, Jamie. We were young and foolish, and it's all in the past. There's no reason we can't get along now."

Jamie inhaled sharply. Foolish to ever get married, or foolish to break up? She didn't dare ask him; she didn't even dare ask herself.

It didn't matter now, anyway, she thought fiercely. All

the same, a flood of jumbled feelings filled her chest, making it hot and tight. She tilted her chin up defiantly. "Seems to me there's every reason. You're doing the same thing now you did then—making major life decisions for me without my permission or knowledge."

Stone took a step toward the door. "I'm sorry you're not happy about this, Jamie. I've recommended what I think is in the best interest of the station, and I came in here to give you some advance notice so you won't be blindsided when Mr. Milton calls you into his office." He crossed the room and turned, his hand on the doorknob. "Since we'll be working together for the next two months, Jamie, I hope we can get along like civilized adults."

Stone closed the door behind him and leaned a hand against it, feeling a lot less sensible than he'd sounded. The fact was, he didn't feel any too civilized himself right now. It had been three years since he'd last seen Jamie, but time had done nothing to lessen her impact on him. His heart had jumped like a jackrabbit when he'd seen her on the air, and when she'd burst through the door of the dressing room, gyrating like a rock star, it had darn near bounded right out of his chest.

She was the same old Jamie, with those same heartbreaker blue eyes, that same fine-textured, wheat-colored hair, those same surprisingly lush curves hidden under her clothes.

And that same intriguing, two-sided personality. It was one of the things he'd loved most about her. In public, she was cool and quiet and reserved, but when she was alone, a whole other side emerged. She could be wild or wacky or wanton, or all three at once. It was the side of her that always came out when they made love.

The thought of it made him ache. He'd never known anything sweeter than Jamie's unbridled passion, and thinking about it now made him crave her like candy.

He'd be better off concentrating on other aspects of Jamie, he upbraided himself—like the way she had no concept of the sacrifices required to build a solid financial future, no real appreciation of money. Probably because she'd always had it. Her tastes might run to blue jeans and country music and she might take pride in supporting herself on her own salary, but she came from a well-heeled family, and he'd do well to remember just how different their backgrounds really were.

Too different for long-term compatibility, as their failed marriage clearly demonstrated.

He heard a thump on the other side of the door and wondered what she was up to. Knowing Jamie, it might be anything. He gave the door a slight push, opening it a faint crack.

"Civilized adults, indeed!" he heard her fume. "I'll show you a civilized adult!"

Stone grinned. He knew he shouldn't, but he couldn't resist. He pushed the door all the way open and peered inside.

Jamie stood facing the door, her eyes crossed, her features scrunched, her fingers wagging from her ears like a rebellious four-year-old. Stone gave a soft chortle—then his gaze slid lower and he realized that the thump he'd heard had been the buttons on the blazer hitting the door. She was once again topless, wearing nothing but a lacy wisp of a bra over her full, white breasts.

"Caught you!"

She uncrossed her eyes and made a grab for the jacket, a flush staining her cheeks. Stone smiled, his gaze riveted on her cleavage. He couldn't resist a parting shot. "By the way, Jamie—your temper's not the only thing that's still hot."

She hurled the jacket at him just as he ducked out the door, looking for all the world like she wished it were a brick.

Yes sir, it was the same old Jamie. And Stone's heart, as well as a few other parts of his anatomy, was having the same old reaction to her.

He rubbed a hand over his chest as he strode down the hall toward the newsroom. If he had any sense at all, he'd keep his distance, physically and emotionally. She'd hurt him more than he'd thought possible, and he didn't need a second helping of pain like that.

There were plenty of women who would welcome his attentions, who would be glad he was ambitious, who would be proud of his accomplishments and not act as if he were committing a federal crime if he worked hard and put in long hours.

So why did he feel this pull of attraction to the one woman who'd flat-out rejected him, who clearly didn't want him, who'd cut him out of her life?

Stone shook his head in self-disgust. He must be a glutton for punishment. Why else would he have taken this second-rate job at a fifth-rate station out in the boondocks? Hell, he'd even reshuffled his schedule and put off better-paying clients in larger markets in order to accept this assignment. He'd told himself it was because he wanted to tackle a station with rural demographics, but even he hadn't bought the excuse.

No. He'd taken this job because he'd heard Jamie was working here, and he hadn't been able to resist the idea of seeing her again. He knew that full well. What he didn't know was why.

Maybe he'd thought seeing her again might get her out of his system. Maybe he'd subconsciously hoped it would give him a sense of closure and allow him to finally get on with his life. Maybe he'd thought that Jamie in the flesh couldn't possibly be as compelling as the Jamie who haunted his memory, who had his love life locked in cold storage except for the times she woke him in the middle of the night to make him toss and turn and ache and burn.

Maybe it was nothing so profound or positive. Maybe, he thought wryly as he pushed open the newsroom door, he was like a battered prize-fighter who just couldn't accept the fact he'd lost the match and insisted on going another round. Maybe he needed to have his heart pummeled and beaten and bruised until it simply stopped beating for her.

Whatever the reason, he was here. And he hoped he would finally find a way to get her out from under his skin, once and for all.

Chapter Two

"Hi there, Lulu." Jamie pulled the front door of her grandmother's house closed behind her and bent to rub the ears of Grams's large calico cat, who purred loudly as she brushed against Jamie's ankles. Judging from the muffled blare of the television and the fragrant, familiar aroma wafting in the air, Grams was in the kitchen, simultaneously cooking and watching her favorite talk show.

Jamie straightened and pulled off her jacket, wishing she hadn't accepted her grandmother's dinner invitation. She had no appetite, not even for her grandmother's famous chicken cacciatore. Her stomach was still in knots from her encounter with Stone and the long afternoon of contract negotiations that had followed.

As Stone had warned, the station's general manager had insisted on making her the new anchor. Whether she liked it or not, she was going to be on the air for the next two months. Her only consolation was that she'd succeeded in making the new contract conditional. After the sweeps period was over, she'd get her old job back if she still hated anchoring the news. She'd also managed to get a commitment that the station would let her produce a weekly segment to help hard-to-adopt children find homes.

The whole negotiation process had been an ordeal, and one of the hardest parts had been sitting across the table from Stone. He made her feel all torn up inside, raw and rattled and restless.

And angry. Furious, in fact. True, he'd helped her get the two concessions in her contract, but that was hardly to his credit. Considering that the whole situation was his fault, it was the least he could do. How dare he come barreling back into her life and throw her entire career into chaos?

Not just her career, she thought ruefully, hanging her blazer on the coatrack in the hall. Her state of mind. Seeing Stone again made her feel as unsettled as a sailboat in a tornado. He, on the hand, seemed maddeningly unaffected.

Maybe it was just stubborn pride, but she hated to think he was over her so completely. Not that she wasn't over him, she told herself; she was. She *was*.

Jamie followed Lulu to the kitchen, where she found her grandmother absently tearing leaves of lettuce into a large wooden bowl, raptly peering over the top of her wire-rim glasses at the television on the baker's rack against the wall. The tiny gray-haired woman started when Jamie entered the room, then shoved her glasses higher on her nose and beamed. "Well, if it isn't the new TV star!" She wiped her hands on her gingham apron, reached for the remote control and zapped off the television before flinging her thin arms around Jamie and squeezing with surprising force. "I'm so proud of you I could burst my buttons!"

Jamie returned her grandmother's hug. Grams was a television junkie, starstruck by anyone who appeared on the screen. She'd phoned Jamie after the newscast, as excited as a quiz show contestant at seeing her granddaughter on television, and issued the dinner invitation. Grams couldn't understand why Jamie didn't view her new role at the station as a godsend, and she even seemed to think the fact that Stone was back in town was good news.

"You won't feel that way if I start stuttering on the air, Grams."

Grams reached up and patted her cheek. "Shucks, child, you haven't stuttered in years. You're over it. This might be exactly what you need to convince yourself."

So much for sympathy, Jamie thought wryly. But then, she should have known what response to expect from her eternally optimistic grandmother. Jamie shook her head and smiled fondly. "You're worse than any stage mother in history."

"No stage mother ever had such talent to crow about." Grams gave Jamie another squeeze before she released her. "Why, even that old crotchety Mrs. Hutchison said you came across as likeable. And Harriett Myerson said when you started crying over that story about those poor children, she started crying herself. Myrtle Crevins thought you looked dignified—like a younger version of Dianne Sawyer!"

Jamie picked a piece of carrot out of the salad, a smile playing across her lips despite her distress at the situation. Grams had probably spent the better part of the day burning up the phone lines with her cronies.

"Agnes called her entire ladies' club and told them to watch, then phoned them again to get them to call the station."

Jamie froze, a strip of green pepper poised in the air. "Call the station? You mean the TV station?"

Grams covered her mouth with her hand. "Oops! I didn't mean to let that slip."

Jamie braced herself against the counter, her shoulders tensed. "What are you talking about, Grams? Why did Agnes call the station?"

Grams turned and fussed with a pan on the stove. "Well, I have a little PR experience—I used to be in charge of publicity for the literary club, you know—and after I saw you on the show this morning, I thought you could use a little help."

Oh, crimony. Jamie crossed the kitchen and grasped her

grandmother's hands. "Grams, what are you talking about? What did you do?"

Grams shrugged. "Nothing, really. I just arranged for a few of my friends to call the station and say how much we liked you."

Jamie stiffened. "You didn't."

Grams's eyes held a mischievous gleam. "I'm afraid we did. We said how much we liked you and what a pleasure it was to see such a pretty face on the screen and how we hoped they'd make you the newsgirl for good."

Jamie dropped her hands and groaned. "Oh, Grams..."

Grams's brow knit in concern. "I did it before I talked to you, honey. I didn't know you didn't want to be on TV. You did such a nice job and looked so lovely I thought I'd give your career a little boost."

Jamie strode across the kitchen, picked up the phone and held it out to her grandmother. "Grams, I want you to call the station right now and tell Stone what you've done," she said sternly.

Grams turned to the stove to stir the tomato sauce. "I can't do that, honey."

"Why not?"

"Because he's not at the station."

Whenever Grams used that innocent tone, she was anything but. Jamie narrowed her eyes suspiciously. "And just how do you know that?"

"Because he's on his way over here. After you told me he was in town, I called and invited him to dinner."

Jamie hung up the phone with a clatter. "Grams! How could you?"

"Well, why on earth not? I figured he could use a good home-cooked meal."

"Why not? I'll tell you why not. In the first place, he's my ex-husband and I have no interest in socializing with him. Our relationship is over, finished, kaput." Jamie sliced the air with her hand. "Secondly, he's forcing me to do something I hate, and look ridiculous doing, with no regard whatsoever for my feelings. Thirdly, and most importantly, he's ruining my career. No one in town will take me seriously as a producer once this ridiculous little stint at the anchor desk is over.''

Grams continued stirring. ''That's still no reason to begrudge him a home-cooked meal,'' she said mildly.

Jamie narrowed her eyes. ''I know what you're up to, Grams, and it won't work. Besides, for all you know, he's got a wife and kid by now.''

''He doesn't. I asked.''

The words stopped Jamie cold. Her knees felt suddenly unsteady and she leaned against the counter as an inexplicable wave of relief surged through her. Something else, something warm and fuzzy, fluttered in her chest.

Her fingers tightened on the Formica countertop as she tried to batten down the feeling. Stone's marital status didn't affect her in any way. She didn't have any illusions about them ever getting back together. Their marriage was over and done with, and she really shouldn't care.

But she did.

Nonsense, she told herself. She just didn't want him remarrying before she did, that was all. Besides, she was furious with him and in no mood to be wishing him a happy home life.

She pushed off the counter. ''Grams, you can just drop all the matchmaking schemes. Stone and I aren't getting back together.''

Grams's eyes were wide and innocent. ''Who said anything about matchmaking? I'm just trying to be neighborly.'' Her self-satisfied smile said otherwise. ''But he was mighty interested to hear that you weren't involved with anyone, either.''

Jamie's stomach did a flip-flop just as a knock sounded on the door. Grams turned back to the pan on the stove, tending it as though it suddenly required urgent attention. ''There he is now. Could you let him in, dear?''

Jamie strode to the door and yanked it open to find Stone leaning on the doorjamb. He held a bottle of wine in one hand and wore a leather jacket that exactly matched the soft mocha of his eyes. He looked rugged and rakish and entirely too appealing. Jamie scowled at him. "I can't believe you had the nerve to come over here."

"My, my. What a warm greeting." Stone smiled as he eased open the screen door. "I take it your grandmother didn't tell you she'd invited me to dinner?"

"Did she tell *you* she'd invited *me?*"

"No, but I figured she would. Especially after the grilling about my personal life."

Jamie winced. "And you accepted, anyway?"

"I'm too fond of your grandmother to turn her down. Besides, we have to work together, Jamie, so we might as well get used to being around each other."

He grinned as he stepped inside, brushing against her in the process. Despite her irritation, the contact sent a skitter of warmth racing through her and she stepped back as though she'd been burned. Strictly a biological reaction, Jamie told herself. After all, sex had always been heated between them. Her body had no conscience, no power of reason—just memory.

Great, just great. Just what she needed—her body responding to Stone like Pavlov's dog to a bell.

"Well, hello there, Lulu. Long time, no see." Stone bent and stroked the enormous cat, who was rubbing against his leg and purring like a motorboat. "I'm glad someone around here is glad to see me." He straightened and headed for the kitchen, making himself right at home as though three years hadn't elapsed at all. Jamie felt her shoulders tense, hating the fact he unnerved her so.

She trailed into the kitchen after him and found him hoisting Grams off her feet in a bear hug. Sweeping women off their feet seemed to be his stock-in-trade, she thought hotly. It was certainly what he'd done to her when they'd met.

Well, she had her feet planted firmly back on the ground now, and she was going to give Stone a good dose of reality, too.

"Grams has something to tell you, Stone," Jamie

prompted, giving her grandmother a meaningful look as he set her down.

"In a moment, Jamie. Let's get our guest something to drink first. Why don't you open that nice bottle of wine he brought?"

"Stone's not a guest. He's..." Jamie stopped abruptly. What was she going to say? *Family?* He certainly wasn't that anymore. *Unwelcome?* That was more like it. She turned her back and yanked open a drawer. "He's been here often enough that he doesn't need special treatment." She slammed the drawer and opened another. "Where the heck to do you keep the corkscrew, Grams?"

"I'll get it." Stone stepped beside her, close enough to brush her sleeve, and extracted a corkscrew from the back of the drawer. "Just where I remembered it." He blew a spot of dust off the handle and turned to Grams. "As I recall, Flossie, you like to serve wine on special occasions. I take it there haven't been many of those around here in a while."

"I don't believe in drinking when folks are depressed, and there hasn't been much cause to celebrate," Grams replied.

Oh, wonderful, Grams, Jamie inwardly moaned. Make the man think I've been pining away for him! She shot her grandmother a warning look and pulled three glasses from the shelf, plunking them down on the counter so hard she nearly broke their stems.

Stone rinsed the corkscrew in the sink, then expertly uncorked the bottle.

"We need a toast," Grams said when he'd filled the glasses. "Stone, you were always good at those."

He held up his glass and grinned, first at Grams, then at Jamie. "To old friends and new beginnings."

"I don't like anything about these new beginnings," Jamie hissed.

"Then just drink to the first part of the toast. To old friends." He saluted Jamie with his glass, then tipped it to his lips.

The words made Jamie chafe. They'd been more than friends to each other—a lot more. They'd been man and wife, joined together in holy matrimony, as close as two people could be. How could he discount that?

Because he'd never taken their marriage as seriously as she had, she told herself. If he had, he never would have put his career ahead of her needs.

Grams was watching her intently. Determined not to give herself away, Jamie took a sip, but the lump in her throat made it hard to swallow.

So that was all they were in his eyes now—old friends. He was over her so completely that he viewed her platonically. Well, that certainly explained how he could just breeze back into her life as though nothing had ever happened between them.

She wished she could say the same. If they'd been just friends, he never would have managed to break her heart and it wouldn't be pounding so hard now. For that matter, she wouldn't be comparing every man she met to him, and they wouldn't all come up lacking.

Old friends, indeed! Jamie set her glass down so hard that some of the wine sloshed on the white countertop. Stone picked up a dishcloth just as Jamie reached for a paper towel, and their fingers collided over the spill. Jamie stared at their hands, both poised to mop up the mess but getting in each other's way, both hesitating, both waiting for the other to make the first move.

It reminded her of the end of their marriage.

She jerked back and let Stone deal with the spill alone. "Okay, Grams, you've stalled long enough. Let's not celebrate under false pretenses. Tell Stone what you did this morning."

Grams cocked her head at Stone as he carried the wine-drenched washcloth to the sink. "I watched Jamie on the news, and I thought she did a jam-up job. I was proud as punch."

"Get to the point, Grams."

Ignoring her granddaughter, Grams gave Stone a winsome smile. "I thought she did such a spectacular job, Stone, that I called up all my friends and urged them to phone the station and say how much they liked her."

Stone's mouth quirked in a smile. He wrung out the cloth and hung it on the sink, then turned to face the elderly woman. "Did you, now?"

Grams nodded, her eyes downcast. "'Fraid so. You've been sandbagged."

Stone lounged against the counter, his expression amused. "How many friends do you suppose called the station, Flossie?"

Grams shrugged. "I don't know. With Agnes's ladies' club, maybe as many as twenty." She put down the wooden spoon and wiped her hands on her apron. "I was only trying to help Jamie."

Stone smiled, his dimple flashing. "No harm done. It doesn't change a thing."

Jamie jerked forward. "If you hadn't gotten the calls, you'd have no reason to put me on the air."

Stone crossed the room and picked up his wineglass. "Not all the calls were from your grandmother's friends."

"And just how the heck would you know that?"

"There are a couple of clues." Stone turned to Grams. "What is the—ah—age range of the ladies you encouraged to call the station?"

"Oh, my goodness." Grams busily stirred the sauce. "They were all about my age." She pointed the wooden spoon at Stone and gave him a coy grin. "You should know better than to ask a gal how many years she's got under her garters!"

Stone reached out and patted Grams's back. "I wouldn't dream of it. Whatever your age, Flossie, you wear it well."

Oh, brother! Jamie rolled her eyes at the ceiling. He was using his considerable charm, pulling out all the stops and laying it on thick, and Grams was just eating it up. It was positively nauseating.

Stone turned to Jamie. "To answer your question, I took

dozens of the calls myself, and many of the callers were quite young.''

Jamie's palms grew damp. "But you can't tell a person's age over the telephone! Lots of elderly ladies—'' she cast an apologetic glance at her grandmother, who'd always resented the term ''—sorry, Grams—can sound young on the phone.''

"Maybe so.'' Stone took a sip of wine, eyeing her over the rim. "But not many of them can sound like men.'' His eyes held a glimmer of amusement. She realized she was staring at him open-mouthed and quickly clamped her lips together. "Besides, the station received more than a hundred calls.''

One hundred people had called to say they liked her on the air? She'd never known Stone to lie, but the figure was outrageous. "You're making that up.''

"Jamie Lee Erickson! Where are your manners?'' Grams scolded.

Stone shrugged. "If you don't believe me, you can check with the newsroom secretary.''

She could—and would. But he wouldn't have recommended it as a course of action if he were trying to dupe her. "Maybe Grams's friends called several times—or encouraged other people to call.''

"Oh, they wouldn't have done that. They're not underhanded enough to think like that.'' Grams looked at Stone and chortled. "I am, though. I wish I'd thought of it!''

Jamie stifled a groan. Her grandmother had clearly defected to the enemy camp. Jamie was anxious to get the meal over with so she could escape to the peace and quiet of her own home, where no one was trying to manipulate her, away from Stone's disturbing presence and her grandmother's blatant matchmaking efforts.

She turned and abruptly picked up the salad. "I'll help you put dinner on the table, Grams.''

"That was a delicious meal, Flossie.'' Stone drained his coffee cup and cast another glance at Jamie. She'd been stiff and silent throughout dinner, barely picking at her food, her spine perfectly aligned with the back of her chair. It was a sure sign Jamie was upset; the more agitated she became, the more erect her posture grew. Right now she looked like a candidate for the Marine Corps honor guard.

Another indication was the untouched slice of chocolate silk pie on her plate. Jamie was a certifiable chocoholic, and he'd never known her to leave a bite of anything chocolate on her plate, much less an entire serving of her grandmother's homemade dessert.

"Thank you, Stone. I got the sauce recipe from the Cantering Cook show on channel twelve..."

Stone pretended to listen to Flossie's rambling chatter with the same polite interest he'd feigned throughout the meal. The truth was, he'd had a hard time taking his eyes off Jamie long enough to follow any of Flossie's prattle about soap operas and talk shows.

Despite her obvious displeasure at his presence, he felt a familiar tug of attraction toward her. Jamie was just as lovely as the day they'd met. No, lovelier. Then she'd been twenty-two and fresh out of college, just barely an adult, and now she was clearly all woman. He'd been the news director at a station in Tulsa, and she'd been a production assistant for the Boffo the Clown show, and he'd fallen for her hard and fast. She was bright and funny and warm— not to mention the sexiest woman he'd ever met.

He'd known they came from different backgrounds, but at the time it hadn't seemed to matter; all that mattered was being with her. When he married her, he'd made up his mind to work hard and build a solid career and make sure she never wanted for anything.

Which ended up being the very reason she left him.

He'd been a fool to think anything lasted forever. With his experience in contract negotiations, he should have know better. As it turned out, marriage contracts were even more easily broken than business ones.

What had ever made him think a country bumpkin from

the wrong side of the tracks could figure out how to make a woman like Jamie happy, anyway?

He glanced at her again, trying to pinpoint exactly what it was about her that had changed. Her slightly uptilted nose, her full, lush lips, her soft blond hair...all were just as he remembered. The difference was in her eyes. They were still wide, still framed with a soft sweep of long, dark lashes, still that incredible shade of pansy blue—but now there was an edge, a certain wariness in her gaze. Was it a permanent feature, or did he bring it out in her?

She was furious with him, that was for sure. He rubbed his jaw. Maybe that wasn't entirely bad. At least it meant he could still stir a strong emotion in her. The one thing he couldn't have stood from her was indifference. Because heaven only knew she stirred up a maelstrom in him.

When he'd seen her on the air that morning, his pulse had skyrocketed, and the blood had roared in his ears. It had been difficult to stay in his seat and maintain a normal demeanor in front the station's executives. Here he was, the highly credentialed, highly touted and even more highly paid consultant they'd brought in to save their station from it's dead-last and sinking position, and all he wanted to do was dash down the hall, interrupt the newscast and kiss his wife until she kissed him back.

Correction: ex-wife. Funny how he had a hard time remembering that, how he still thought of her as his wife, even after all this time.

His wife who had left him. A nerve ticked in his jaw, and he wiped his mouth with his napkin to hide it. After all this time he should be over it, but it was an emotional wound that hadn't healed.

Well, he'd be damned if he ever let her know it. And he'd be double damned if he let her make him lose his composure—or his company's track record. He'd managed to improve the ratings at every station that had contracted his consulting services so far and he didn't intend to stop now. Success was the key to the financial security he'd dreamed of all his life.

The financial security he'd once wanted for his wife and the family they would someday have together.

A wave of bitterness rose in his throat and he swallowed it back. He couldn't afford to think about that now, couldn't afford to dwell on what was over and done.

He needed to figure out how to gain her cooperation. It was going to be difficult working with her if she didn't cool down. Was she upset because of his recommendation that she be made an anchor, or was her wrath more personal in nature? He needed to find out.

Stone pushed back his chair. "Why don't you go on into the living room and relax, Flossie? Jamie and I will deal with the dishes."

"Why, thank you, Stone." Grams gave him a wide grin and a wink. "I believe I will. After all, it's time for my favorite detective show."

Stone grinned in amusement. The old gal's matchmaking scheme was entirely transparent. The scowl on Jamie's face indicated she thought so, too, and was less than appreciative of her grandmother's efforts.

Stone pulled out Flossie's chair, then moved behind Jamie, intending to extend her the same courtesy, but she abruptly scooted back and nearly nailed his toe with her chair leg. She jerked to her feet and began snatching dishes off the table, clanking Grams's silverware into a pile atop the china.

Stone reached for the stack of plates in her hands. "You'd better let me take these, Jamie. At the rate you're going, there won't be any dishes left to wash."

She looked up, her gaze as sharp as broken glass. "I have half a mind to throw these at you."

Stone forced a smile and an easy tone. "I'm sorry you're angry, Jamie. I wish you wouldn't take this personally."

"How else am I supposed to take it?" She shoved the plates at him and turned away, picking up a platter of pasta and charging to the kitchen.

He followed behind her. "My recommendation today

was purely a business decision. It had nothing to do with us."

"You expect me to believe that?"

"What do you think I'm doing—making you an anchor to torture you?"

"Something like that." She plopped the platter on the counter and whirled around.

He was right behind her when she turned, and some primitive reflex made him place both hands on either side of her, pinning her against the counter. His pelvis bumped against hers, and a jolt of attraction, rash and raw and shocking in its sheer impact, pulsed through him. "If I were looking for a way to torture you, Jamie, I'd come up with something far more interesting."

She gazed up at him, her eyes the color of deep water. He saw her pupils dilate and darken, and he knew the exact moment she felt it, too, felt the inexorable pull of attraction.

Her lips parted and the tip of her tongue darted out to moisten them. He leaned toward her, hungry to claim those lips, anxious, aching to feel the full length of her pressed against him again. The memory of her body, of its perfect fit against his, flashed through his mind in vivid Technicolor. The years that had passed, the events that had happened since he'd last been with her seemed suddenly meaningless. The intervening portion of his life had been nothing more than the marking of time until he was with her again.

Her chest rose and fell like the breast of a frightened bird, her breasts pushing against him with every breath. He gazed down at her, at her half-closed lids, helpless to stop himself even though he knew he'd probably regret what he was about to do.

He dipped his head and grazed her lips with his own. He'd forgotten how soft her mouth was, how sweet and ripe it felt. His lips settled more fully over hers, drawing her bottom lip into his mouth, and she gave a little moan. The familiar sound drove him over the edge and he drew her to him, plundering her mouth with his tongue. Desire and a deeper, more dangerous emotion he didn't dare name raged through him.

He'd thought he was over that. Over *her*. He was on treacherous ground, he was sinking in quicksand, and if he didn't stop now, he'd be over his head and drowning.

He drew back, stunned at the intensity of his reaction. He gazed at her a moment longer, at her uptilted face, at the curve of her lashes against her closed lids, at her willing, tempting, kiss-swollen mouth, then turned and stalked back into the dining room. He picked up a water glass and drained the contents, wishing for something stronger.

Lord Almighty, what had he done? He'd come here tonight to smooth things over, to normalize their relationship so they could work together, and he'd acted like a caveman. He'd forgotten his responsibility to the station, forgotten about amicable work relationships, forgotten everything except how she looked and felt and smelled and tasted and how much he wanted her.

Even worse, he'd forgotten how things stood between them—that they were divorced, that she had left him, that she didn't want him, didn't even want to be in the same room with him.

But she *had* wanted to kiss him. What the hell was he supposed to make of that?

Stone ran a hand down his face and swore, wishing he could just walk out the door. It was no solution, of course. He'd have to face her tomorrow, and he didn't want to have a confrontation in the newsroom. Besides, he'd been the one to suggest clearing the dishes, and he always followed through on his commitments. Heaving a sigh, he headed back to he kitchen.

He found her standing at the sink, staring out the darkened window, her silky hair streaming down her back. He thrust his hands into the pockets of his khakis. "Jamie, we need to talk."

She turned on the faucet and busily rinsed a plate, deliberately avoiding his gaze, not wanting him to see how her face was burning. She couldn't believe she'd fallen under his spell like that, couldn't believe how easily she'd kissed him, couldn't believe how badly she'd wanted to. She felt dizzy and flustered, and tried to hide her confusion by attempting to muster some of her earlier anger. "No, Stone. *I* need to talk. *You* need to listen." She shut off the faucet and whipped around, clenching a dish towel. "You might be the station's consultant and you might be able to make a fool of me at work, but you can't do it outside the newsroom. I won't stand for it."

"If anyone's a fool, it's me."

She glanced at his face and saw no trace of mockery or amusement.

"I'm sorry, Jamie."

She had to admit that he looked it. His eyes were sad and solemn, his mouth a flat, firm line. For some reason, the thought that Stone was sorry he'd kissed her did nothing to make her feel better.

He paused and cleared his throat, running his hand through his thick dark hair. "I apologize. I don't know what happened. It must have been some kind of flashback."

"Like a bad war experience? How very flattering."

"There was never anything bad about the physical part of our relationship."

It was true. Things would be a lot easier now if there had been, but that part had always been pure magic. Passion had always blazed between them at the slightest provocation—a touch, a word, a look—like a match to dry kindling. Sometimes all it took was a thought. She used to think they were sexually telepathic.

Jamie picked up a plate and jammed it into the dishwasher, wedging it unevenly between the wire brackets. Turning back to the sink, she picked up a nylon scouring pad and attacked a Teflon dish. "The key word in that statement is *was*."

"I'll try to keep it in mind." He crammed his hands in his pockets. "I guess old habits die hard."

Old habit? Was that what she was to him? She liked that

even less than the ''old friend'' and ''flashback'' comments.

''Let's just forget about it, Stone.'' She squirted a stream of dishwashing liquid into the pan, filling the room with the soapy scent of lemon, knowing she stood a better chance of forgetting her own name than forgetting that kiss and the shattering effect it had on her.

She couldn't let Stone bulldoze his way back into her life like this. She'd fought too hard and too long to get over him, to get past the pain of their failed marriage, to build a fresh start for herself. She couldn't—wouldn't—let him gain an emotional foothold again.

She needed to fight him on this anchor issue, not just for the sake of her career, but for her self-esteem as well. She needed to prove to herself that he no longer had any power over her, that he couldn't hurt her in any way, that every tie between them had been severed.

''I'll finish clearing the table,'' he said, heading back into the dining room.

She attacked the soapy dish with a vengeance. Somehow, someway, she had to get out of that contract and off the air. Somehow, someway, she had to get free of Stone, once and for all.

Chapter Three

Jamie stared at the notepad on her desk, trying to tune out the bustle of the newsroom around her and focus her thoughts. She needed to develop a plan for the adoption series, but she was still too jittery from delivering the morning newscast to think straight. Her second day in front of the camera had been no easier than her first; once again she'd had to concentrate like crazy to keep her terror at bay, and now she felt frazzled and exhausted.

She had to figure out a way to get off the air. She'd considered deliberately doing a bad job reading the news, but in order to do that, she'd have to think about her delivery—and if she thought about how she sounded instead of what she was saying, she was likely to start stuttering.

Which was the whole reason she wanted off the air in the first place. It was a catch-22 situation.

Jamie rubbed her forehead, trying to alleviate the headache that was building like a thundercloud, the result of too much stress and too little sleep. She'd tossed and turned all night, keyed up over the job and Stone's reappearance in her life.

The thought of Stone made her head throb harder, and

she opened her desk to extract a tin of aspirin. The encounter in the kitchen had replayed like a looped tape, and she'd spent long, sleepless hours castigating herself for it. How could she have responded so heatedly, so rapidly, so embarrassingly *thoroughly* to a man with a track record for breaking her heart—a man who was once again in the process of turning her life upside down?

But then, she'd always had a strong physical response to Stone, ever since she first laid eyes on him. Jamie popped two aspirin in her mouth and washed them down with a swig of cola, giving a heavy sigh.

Had it really been four years ago? It seemed like yesterday that she'd sought him out in the newsroom in Tulsa, eager to talk him into covering Boffo the Clown's participation in a benefit for disabled children. She'd been green as grass about the news industry and had naively wandered into the control room just as the five-o'clock show hit the air.

The memory of how he'd looked was burned in her mind like a brand. She could still see his loosened tie, still see the chest hair curling out over the single undone button of his shirt, still see the way his five-o'clock shadow deepened the cleft in his chin. His dark, wavy hair had been in need of a trim and had curled over his collar, and his sleeves had been rolled up, exposing strong, tanned arms. He'd silenced her with a look and a slashing-his-throat gesture, and she'd stood still as a statue for the next fifteen minutes, watching him supervise two live, remote broadcasts. Everything about him had seemed masculine, powerful, larger than life, and he'd made her insides quiver like jelly. The intensity of his concentration as he focused on his work had been the sexiest thing she'd ever seen.

Funny how the very thing that had first attracted her was the very thing that later drove them apart.

A shadow fell across the paper in front of her and jerked Jamie out of her reverie. Todd Dodson loomed over her, his pasty face contorted into an ominous scowl.

"Well, well, if it isn't Little Miss Opportunist." His lips

curled into a sneer. "I'm sure you'll understand if I don't congratulate you on your promotion, won't you, Jamie?"

"Todd…" Oh, dear. From the look of his bloodshot eyes and the reek of stale booze on his breath, he'd been on a real bender. Jamie reflexively scooted her chair away from him. "Todd, I'm so sorry. I tried to call you over and over again yesterday morning. When I couldn't reach you, I didn't know what to do."

"You obviously figured it out pretty quickly." The words came out in a snarl of sarcasm. "You really pulled a fast one on me."

Jamie gazed up at him, pulling her brows together in bewilderment. "I don't know what you mean."

"Oh, come on, Jamie. You sold me down the river. You could have covered for me, could have said I called in with car trouble or something. But instead, you stole my job right out from under me. Thanks to you, I've been bumped down to the reporter pool."

She'd seen him in ugly moods before—mornings when he'd been so hungover he could hardly function, mornings when she'd had to ply him with aspirin and black coffee, mornings when she'd personally applied his makeup because his hands shook so badly—but she'd never seen him as angry as he was now. The raw hostility in his voice sent a frisson of fear shimmying down her spine. She strove to maintain a calm expression and reached out her hand to give his arm a reassuring pat. "Todd, I'm so sorry. I promise you I didn't do this on purpose."

"Liar." Todd spat out the word like rotten fruit and jerked away from her touch, then leaned down until his face was a few scant, odiferous inches from hers. His breath assaulted her senses. "You've ruined my career, and I'm not going to let you get away with it. Mark my words, Jamie—I'll get you for this." He narrowed his eyes into a final, menacing leer before he straightened and stalked across the newsroom.

Jamie sank back in her chair, her heart pounding wildly.

She'd never had so much blatant anger directed at her in her life, and she'd certainly never before been threatened.

Her fingers ached, and she realized she was gripping the arm of her chair so tightly her knuckles had turned white. She folded her hands in her lap and rubbed them as she drew a deep breath and closed her eyes, willing herself to relax.

"What did Todd want?"

Jamie's eyes flew open. Stone stood before her, his eyes wary as they followed Todd's retreating back. Jamie swallowed, her mind racing.

If she told Stone the truth, he wouldn't just bump Todd to the reporter pool—he'd fire him altogether. Mr. Milton had given Stone complete control of the newsroom. She didn't want that on her conscience. She felt terrible about taking Todd's job as it was. Besides, she was certain his threats were harmless. When he cooled down and she explained the situation, she was sure he'd understand.

She drew in a deep lungful of air and tried to act nonchalant. "Nothing. We were just talking."

Stone's eyebrow shot into a dubious curl. "I bet you were. And from the ugly look on his face, I bet I can guess the topic." He settled himself on the edge of her desk and rested a stack of papers on his lap. "Todd was none too happy about his reassignment. If he gives you a hard time, Jamie, you let me know."

His concern unnerved her. Jamie pulled herself erect in her chair and tried to hide her reaction under a show of bravado. "I can handle Todd. What I want to know is who should I notify if *you* give me a hard time?"

Stone's eyes darkened and his lips firmed into a serious line. He leaned forward, his forearm braced on his thigh, his fingers wrapped around the papers in his hand. "Look, Jamie—I'm sorry about last night. I didn't mean to upset you." His eyes searched hers, their expression troubled. "I don't want to do anything you might consider sexual harassment."

Sexual harassment? That was the farthest thought from

her mind. She'd been an all-too-eager participant. Her cheeks burned as she recalled the way she'd pressed herself against him, woven her fingers in his hair and kissed him like there was no tomorrow. If anything, *she'd* sexually harassed *him*. If he hadn't stopped and turned away, no telling how far things would have gone.

Jamie folded her arms protectively across her chest and looked away. "Don't worry about it," she managed to mumble.

Stone hauled himself to his feet. "Well, I'll watch it in the future." His dimple flashed with disturbing appeal. "In fact, I won't touch you again unless you make the first move."

Jamie tried to rally some of her usual spunk. "Don't hold your breath."

His grin widened into a full-fledged smile, the kind that always made her insides quiver, a smile that dusted up memories of all the times she'd initiated their lovemaking. She hadn't been at all bashful about making the first move in their marriage. That spark in his eyes told her he, too, remembered.

He lightly thumped her desk with the papers. "Well, now that we've gotten that settled—here's some fan mail for you."

"Fan mail? Get out of here, Johnson."

"You think I'm kidding? Take a look." He plopped a stack of faxes and hand-delivered letters on the desk in front of her.

Jamie riffled through them, a sense of distress growing with every letter she scanned. Invitations to join organizations, requests for autographed photographs, invitations to speak at luncheons, suggestions for self-serving news stories—more than a dozen messages in all, all from strangers who wanted something from her.

"Look at this," Jamie said, gingerly holding up a sheet of lined notebook paper that reeked of cheap men's cologne. "This guy wants to take me on a date!"

Stone took the paper from her and scanned the letter,

then glanced up. "He must be a real winner. What kind of jerk sends a mash note to someone he doesn't even know and pours an entire bottle of dime-store cologne all over it to boot?"

Was he implying that only a jerk would be interested in her? Jamie immediately jumped to the guy's defense. "I think it's kind of sweet."

Stone's forehead creased into a frown. "You're not thinking about going out with this goon, are you?"

Something made her egg him on. She gave a casual shrug. "Maybe. Why not?"

"Because he might be some sort of a psycho, for Pete's sake. There are some real weirdos out there, Jamie, and people on television are all too often their targets."

Jamie snatched the letter out of his hands. "If you're so worried about it, then take me off the air."

"You know I can't do that. But you need to be careful."

His brows knit together and his eyes narrowed with concern. Funny how the sight made her stomach flutter, how it managed to make her feel all warm inside. A man hadn't cared about her like this since—

Since Stone. Nostalgia as sharp and sweet as a prickly pear blossom assailed her, making it difficult to breathe. No one had ever made her feel more loved, more cherished, more important than Stone had in the early days of their marriage. He'd asked her opinion on everything, really listened to what she'd had to say and remembered what she'd told him. He used to call her in the middle of the day just to hear her voice, used to slip love notes in her purse, used to clip news articles he thought might interest her, used to leave chocolate kisses on her pillow. Life together had been as warm and sunny as a summer afternoon.

But then they'd relocated to Phoenix and his career had claimed all of his attention, clouding out the joy. He'd go to work in the morning while she was still asleep and not come home until after the late-night newscast. He'd spend the better part of every weekend at the station and even when he was home, he was buried in paperwork. Bit by bit, he had become exactly the type of man she'd vowed never to get involved with: a workaholic like her father. The last thing she wanted was a life like her mother's—a life of disappointment and emptiness and early widowhood, all because the man she'd married was so consumed with making money and achieving status that he wouldn't make time to take care of his own health, much less his wife or daughter.

Stone was still standing in front of her. A fresh surge of anger pulsed through her, both for the way he'd let their marriage disintegrate and the predicament he was forcing her into now. But most of all she was angry that he'd made her remember the good times.

She folded the letter and crammed it back into the envelope. "I can take care of myself just fine, thank you." She held up the rest of her mail. "So what am I supposed to do with these?"

"I'll get you copies of the form letters the other anchors send. As for the photo requests—I've already made an appointment for you to have a publicity still made this afternoon. After the image consultant finishes with you, that is."

Alarm bells went off in her head. Jamie sat bolt upright in her chair. "Image consultant? What the heck are you talking about?"

"It's standard procedure to send new on-air personalities to a professional for advice on clothes and hair and makeup. You know that, Jamie."

Oh, she knew, all right. She knew enough to know she didn't like it one little bit. "I happen to like the way I look just fine."

His gaze traveled over her appreciatively, and her skin warmed under his scrutiny. "I do, too, Jamie. I always have." His voice was like crushed velvet, both soft and roughly textured. "But a consultant can give you a more professional look."

Professional? What exactly did *that* mean? One of those every-strand-in-place, sprayed-into-a-helmet hair jobs and makeup applied with a spatula? She thrust out her chin and folded her arms across her chest. "I don't want to be made over."

"Now, Jamie..."

"Hey, Mr. Johnson!" The assignment editor yelled across the room. "We've got two stories breaking and only one crew in the vicinity. Which do you want to cover—a three-alarm fire or an overturned semi on the interstate?"

"I'll be right there," Stone called, pushing off the desk. He gave Jamie a look that said he meant business. "This is a nonnegotiable subject, Jamie. You're to meet with the consultant in the studio dressing room in an hour, and that's an order."

Jamie stood arrow straight in the center of the dressing room and warily eyed the slight, effeminate man sashaying circles around her.

"Hmm..." murmured the consultant, who introduced himself as Jeffrey Hill but suggested she call him Mr. Jeffrey. He stroked his baby-smooth cheek with a manicured hand and looked her over from head to toe. He was dressed all in black, wore his carefully streaked blond hair pulled back in ponytail and had the kind of tan that spoke of hours under a sunlamp. "Hmm," he repeated.

Jamie shifted uneasily, feeling like a poodle at a pet show. He disappeared behind her back, and Jamie whirled around to keep him in her line of vision. He wagged his finger at her in a gesture of disapproval. "No, no, stand perfectly still. I need to look at you from all angles."

"Unless the cameraman is having a really bad day, my backside will never be on the screen," she groused. "Can't we just get this over with?"

Mr. Jeffrey placed his hands on his hips and drew the corners of his Kewpie-doll mouth into a pouty frown. "Now, now, Ms. Erickson. We want to do a thorough job, don't we?"

Jamie bit back a sharp retort concerning what "we" really thought of the matter.

"Do a very thorough job, Jeffrey," came a deep, familiar voice.

Jamie whipped around to see Stone lounging against the door frame, his arms crossed, one foot casually draped across the other. Her spine drew even taller as a flash of indignation shot through her. "If I'm such a hopeless case, perhaps we shouldn't waste Mr. Jeffrey's time."

"Oh, she's not hopeless," Mr. Jeffrey said earnestly, addressing Stone as if he were the one who had spoken and she were an inanimate object. "There's nothing here that we can't handle."

What am I, chopped liver? Jamie did a slow burn as the man lifted a lock of her hair.

"First of all, the hair has to go. *Snip snip.*" Mr. Jeffrey held his fingers like scissors and feigned a cut about two inches from her scalp, still addressing Stone. "She needs serious hair if you want her to be taken seriously."

"I'm not cutting my hair," Jamie said through clenched teeth, thinking of a couple of things on both of these men she'd like to *snip snip.*

Hot pink spots blazed on each of her cheekbones, and the look in her eye could have fried an egg at forty paces. *Jeez, she was adorable when she was angry.* Stone suppressed a smile and cocked his head to one side, pretending to give her an objective perusal.

The truth was that there was nothing objective about his feelings for her. There never had been. Other people might not consider her a classic beauty, but to him she was the most gorgeous woman on the face of the earth—a fact that had seriously handicapped his romantic life ever since their divorce. He wasn't drawn to anyone who didn't remind him of her, and anyone who reminded him of her was nothing but a poor substitute.

He hadn't realized until he'd kissed her last night what he'd been missing. After the divorce, he'd shut the door on his love life and proceeded to bury himself in work. It had been a long, dry, empty three years. And then he'd kissed her, and it was as if a floodgate had opened. A hot, tumultuous rush of feelings had surged out and swirled around inside him like some kind of damn whirlpool.

She shot him a mutinous glare, and he pretended to be studying her thoughtfully, as if he were weighing Jeffrey's suggestion.

She looked perfect just the way she was. Hell, in his opinion she was perfect when she tumbled out of bed first thing in the morning, all mussed and sleep wrinkled, or when she stepped out of the shower dripping wet. In fact, if he had a nickel for every time in the past three years that he'd fantasized about her in just that condition, he could shut down his consulting firm and live in luxury the rest of his life.

Where Jamie was concerned, he completely lost his head. Which was precisely why he'd decided to follow the standard course of action for new on-air talent and refer her to an image consultant.

It didn't look like she was taking kindly to the notion, though. Stone rubbed his chin thoughtfully. She had a stubborn streak that would make a Missouri mule look like a pushover; if he was going to convince her to cooperate, he'd have to make her think it was her own idea.

He nodded amiably. "I agree with Jamie—leave her hair like it is. Gives her that everyday, average, girl-next-door look." He shifted his stance and shoved his hands in the pockets of his jeans, pretending to be oblivious to the fact that Jamie was glaring at him with all her might. "Tell you what—on second thought, don't do such a thorough job on her, after all. Just add a little spit and polish. Let her keep her ordinary, run-of-the-mill appearance. Now that I think about it, that plain look is probably a big part of her appeal."

He could tell from her outraged expression that his words had hit their mark.

"I didn't know you were a beauty expert in addition to all your other talents," she said through clenched teeth.

"I'm not," he replied mildly. "I'm just an expert at recognizing it when I see it."

And you obviously don't see it when you look at me. The thought made her spirits plummet hard and fast, and she pulled her eyes away to hide her hurt.

Why should it matter what he thought? She didn't want him to find her attractive.

Did she?

She gave herself a mental shake and straightened every inch of her five-foot-five frame. Of course not. She was just experiencing a typical reaction to having her appearance insulted.

All the same, she felt a keen sense of deflation. She lifted her eyes back to his face, determined to hide her injured feelings. "I thought I was supposed to be having a *private* consultation with Mr. Jeffrey." She arched an eyebrow and fixed him with what she hoped was a withering stare. "But since you're so knowledgeable, perhaps you'd like to stick around and pick out shades of eye shadow?"

Stone grinned and placed a hand on the door frame. "Sounds like fun, but I've got to check the five-o'clock news lineup." He turned to Mr. Jeffrey. "Remember what I said—just shine her up a little. We don't want her coming across as too glamorous." He gave Jamie a courtly nod and disappeared down the hallway.

Jamie's fingers curled into fists at her side. What an infuriating man! She didn't know which annoyed her more—the fact he wanted her to see a consultant in the first place, or that he'd told the consultant not to make any drastic changes.

No, she knew exactly what bothered her—the words he'd used to describe her. *Ordinary. Average. Everyday. Run-of-the-mill. Plain.* Why, she had half a mind to really show him.

Mr. Jeffrey unzipped a large leather bag and began pulling out an intimidating array of makeup brushes and products. "Have a seat and we'll get to work," he simpered, waving at a low-backed swivel hair.

Jamie hesitantly seated herself and allowed him to drape a cloth around her neck. "Mr. Jeffrey," she began, "I know Stone said we need to keep my everyday appearance simple, but I'm sure there will be occasions when I'll need a more, er...*sophisticated* look. Could you show me how to do that, too?"

From the look on his face, the man lived for requests like this. He clasped his hands together in a gesture of ecstasy. "Most certainly. I'll totally transform you. Why, when I get finished, you won't even recognize yourself!"

Jamie stifled an urge to wince. "Great!" she managed to say.

Mr. Jeffrey pulled a fishing tackle box from his enormous bag and opened the lid to reveal a vast array of tiny pots and tubes. "This is the heavy artillery," he said with a giggle.

Jamie settled back and gave a satisfied smile. She couldn't wait to see Stone's reaction when she appeared on the air tomorrow painted up like a Las Vegas showgirl. "The heavier, the better. Fire away."

Frowning at her reflection in her bedroom mirror that evening, Jamie leaned closer and stroked on another layer of eyeliner, then stepped back to appraise her appearance. She'd carefully followed Mr. Jeffrey's written instructions and applied all of the products just as he'd demonstrated that afternoon, but with a much heavier hand.

The woman who gazed back at her had sculpted cheekbones, shiny ruby lips and no freckles. But something was wrong. This was not at all the effect she was trying to achieve.

Jamie picked up a jar of cold cream just as the doorbell rang. Holding the large jar in her hand, she padded to the door in stocking feet, still frowning.

"Land o' goshen, Jamie, is that you?" Her grandmother stood on the stoop, holding a covered casserole dish, her mouth open.

"It's me all right," Jamie said grimly, stepping aside to let Grams enter.

"I tried out a new casserole I saw on that TV cooking

show, and the recipe made a mountain, so I thought I'd bring you some," Grams babbled as she walked in the door. She stopped short in the foyer and stared at Jamie under the bright glow of the overhead light fixture. "Land's sake, honey, what have you done to yourself? You look like a movie star!"

Jamie closed the door. "It's worse than that," she grumbled. "I look like a television news anchor."

"More terrible things could happen to a body, though you wouldn't know it from the expression on your face." Grams peered curiously over her glasses. "Want to tell me why you're so upset about it?"

"I want to convince Stone that I'm not anchor material."

Gram's brow furrowed quizzically. "I'm usually a pretty quick study, but I don't follow you on this one."

"Come on into the kitchen. I'll explain it while I wipe off the war paint."

Balancing the cold cream in one hand, Jamie carried the casserole in the other. She placed them on the counter, then sat down at the table across from her grandmother. "Stone had me see an image consultant, then told him not to do anything drastic—not to ruin my average, everyday, ordinary, girl-next-door, run-of-the-mill look. He said I was *plain!*" Saying the words aloud made Jamie's blood boil all over again. She thrust herself out of the chair and paced. "Can you imagine anything more insulting? So I asked the consultant to pull out all the stops, to make me into a regular glamour queen. I wanted to go for overkill." She gestured to her face and rolled her eyes in disgust. "And *this* is what I got."

Grams cocked her head to one side and grinned. "Maybe it's what Stone wanted all along."

She stopped cold and stared at her grandmother. "You mean he used reverse psychology on me?"

Grams lifted her bony shoulders, her elfin face wrinkling into a grin. "Could be."

Had Stone deliberately goaded her into doing exactly what he wanted? A flare of indignation welled up in Jamie's chest. "Why, that sneaky, devious, manipulative snake in the grass..."

"I don't think I'd call him that," Grams said mildly.

"Oh, no? Well, what would you call him?"

Grams shrugged. "Smart, maybe. Someone who knows you, knows what makes you tick."

If Grams were right, that meant Stone had counted on her doing the exact opposite of what he suggested—which meant he was able to read her like a book.

Oh, crimony. Was she really that transparent?

And if she was, did he know how he affected her?

The thought was too humiliating to entertain. Jamie snatched the cold cream off the counter.

"Of all the low-down, underhanded, manipulative stunts to pull," she fumed, unscrewing the lid and scooping out a big glob of the fragrant cream.

How could she have been so naive? Stone had set up a psychological ambush, and she'd fallen for it as guilelessly as Bambi. A fresh burst of indignation shot through her veins, filling her with resolve.

"Two can play at this game, Grams." She angrily slathered cold cream on both cheeks. "Stone needs to be taught a lesson."

"I haven't seen that look on your face since you were four years old and poured Kool-Aid down little Tommy Baker's pants." Grams's eyebrows gathered in a worried frown. "What are you going to do?"

Jamie snatched a paper towel off the roll mounted under the cabinet. "Give Stone a taste of his own medicine."

"And just how are you going to do that?"

A feeling of anticipation began to ease the constriction in her chest. Stone didn't know it, but he might have just handed her the ticket for getting off the air.

Jamie wiped a path through the white goo on her face. "I'm going to reverse his reverse psychology." A secretive smile played at the corner of her lips, causing Grams's worried frown to intensify. "And I'm going to enjoy every minute of it."

Chapter Four

Harold's eyes bulged like a bulldog's when Jamie entered the studio the next morning. "You're goin' on the air like *that?*"

Jamie glanced down at her baggy gray sweatshirt and was stabbed by a moment of doubt. Maybe she'd gone too far. Sloppy clothing and no makeup were one thing, but wearing her hair in pigtails might be pushing it.

She swallowed hard. She wouldn't have gone to the grocery store dressed like this, yet here she was, about to go on television in front of a quarter million viewers.

I've got no choice, she thought fiercely. The only way to get pulled off the air was to take drastic measures.

There was nothing in her contract that stipulated anything about her appearance. She was under no obligation to wear her hair in a certain style or her makeup in a certain way, and she'd be darned if she'd let Stone or any prissy-lipped consultant tell her what to do. It was better to endure a little embarrassment over inappropriate clothing than to humiliate herself by stuttering on the air.

Besides, it was too late now to change her mind—or her attire. The large clock on the studio wall said less than three minutes remained before airtime. She continued making her way across the labyrinth of cables and seated herself at the anchor desk.

Her replacement as morning producer, Rob Estes, glanced up from the teleprompter machine and did a double take. "Holy mackerel, Jamie. Why aren't you dressed?"

"I *am* dressed," she said calmly, clipping the tiny microphone to the neck of her sweatshirt. The faded fabric bunched and sagged under its weight. Jamie readjusted it, with the same results.

"But—but—I thought you were in the dressing room changing..." Rob's eyes were large and wild as he ran both hands through his sandy hair.

Empathy surged through Jamie. She knew from her difficult mornings with Todd how panicked he must feel. "It's okay, Rob," she said gently. "I take full responsibility."

"But—but you can't *do* this..."

"One minute," boomed the director's voice.

"It's your business what you look like," Harold called, "but it's my business how you sound. I need a voice level pronto."

Jamie complied, then glanced at Rob. He was standing stock-still, his boyish face ashen.

"Thirty seconds," called the producer.

"It'll be all right, Rob," Jamie reassured him. "No one expects you to follow me into the dressing room and monitor my every move. I'll see that you don't get into trouble." He remained motionless, and she leveled what she hoped was a stern look at him. "Unless you're so rattled you can't manage to run the teleprompter for me."

Her words spurred him to action as the director launched into the final countdown.

Thirty minutes later Jamie unfastened the microphone with a sigh of relief.

"Mr. Johnson's going to kill us," Rob moaned.

"Just leave it to me. I'll deal with him," Jamie said, rising from the set.

She headed for the newsroom, bracing herself for a

showdown. If Stone insisted on making her go on the air tomorrow, she'd show up wearing the same sloppy sweat-shirt—and she'd wear the same thing the next day and the day after *that*, if necessary. If she stood her ground, he'd soon have to capitulate.

The newsroom secretary glanced up and grinned when Jamie entered the room. "Well, if it isn't the most news-worthy person in Texas. You've got the phone lines burn-ing up."

Jamie glanced at the telephone console. Every red button was lit and blinking.

The secretary's smile broadened. "Seems everyone's got something to say about your new casual look."

Jamie cringed. She'd been so focused on Stone's reaction she hadn't given much thought to the public's response. "Who's taking the calls?"

"Stone. He's in his office."

Jamie's heart skipped a beat. "What's his mood?"

"He's a hard one to read, but you'll know soon enough. He wanted to see you as soon as you showed up."

He must be livid, Jamie thought nervously. She paused outside the door to his office, drew a deep breath and knocked.

"Come in."

Stone was seated behind his desk, the phone to his ear, his face shuttered and inscrutable. He motioned for Jamie to enter the room.

"Thanks for your comments," he was saying into the receiver. "We're always interested in the opinions of our viewers, and we'll certainly take your remarks under ad-visement."

He waved a hand toward an armchair. Slowly she low-ered herself to the burgundy leather, her heart pounding.

She wished she could get a handle on what he was think-ing. His expression was as wooden as a fence post. One of the things about him that used to drive her crazy was his incredible reserve, his ability to keep his face deadpan, his emotions hidden.

"Thank you for calling—and thanks for watching channel three news." He hung up the phone and swiveled around to face Jamie, his dimple flashing in a blazing smile. It caught her off guard, and she wrapped her arms protectively across her chest. He must be terribly angry to go to so much trouble to act as if he weren't.

"Well, well, well," he drawled. "If you aren't a sight this morning." He picked up the phone and buzzed the intercom. "Sue, can you handle these calls for a few moments? Just listen, jot down the gist of their comments and get their names and addresses."

He rose from his chair and circled the desk, perching on the edge of it so close to her that his foot nearly brushed her leg. Jamie swallowed nervously, bracing herself for a heated tirade. A shiver ran up her spine and she rubbed her upper arms.

"Jamie, I owe you an apology. I underestimated you." His voice was soft, low and silken. But then, she reminded herself, so was the tail of a tiger.

Jamie cleared her throat and shifted uncomfortably in the chair. This was not the direction she'd expected this conversation to head. She eyed him warily, certain the other shoe was about to drop at any moment.

"Just when I thought I knew all the tricks, along you come with a bagful of new ones. I didn't know you were so savvy about your local market."

She struggled not to fidget. "What—what do you mean?"

Stone smiled again, a slow, lop-sided grin. "I have to admit, when I turned on my set this morning and saw you in that getup, why, I darn near cut my throat." He rubbed his neck. "Of course, I was shaving at the time."

He leaned forward, his hands resting on his thighs, and Jamie's eyes were drawn to the disconcerting way his muscles bulged beneath the taut denim.

Swallowing, Jamie pulled her gaze to his face and lifted her chin. "I was only following your instructions."

Stone narrowed his eyes. "Oh, you were, were you? Are

you saying this…this—'' his gaze swept her from head to toe ''—this *ensemble* is the result of your consultation with Mr. Jeffrey?''

The skepticism in his eyes was unmistakable. Jamie boldly met his gaze. ''Yes, in a way.''

''And what way is that?''

''Well, you said I should look like the girl next door. I think the exact terms you used were 'average, everyday, run-of-the-mill.' So I decided to follow up on your advice.''

Stone stared at her for a moment, then threw back his head and laughed. ''And you were so eager to please me that you went to this extreme? Why, I'm touched at your cooperative spirit.''

His amused tone raised her hackles. Jamie straightened her spine. ''I've been as clear about this as I know how to be, but you don't seem to get the message.'' Her words came out precise and clipped. ''I don't want to be an anchor. I'm not good at it, I'm not right for it, and it's ridiculous of you to try to force me to be something I'm not.''

Stone again settled his hands on his thighs. ''So you tried to prove it. But it didn't work, Jamie.''

He spoke in a calm tone of voice, similar to what an adult might use with a toddler who'd just had a tantrum. Jamie's temper rose to a simmer. Did he think she'd back down if she didn't get a reaction? ''If you think this was an isolated incident, you're mistaken. There's nothing in my contract that says anything about how I have to look. I intend to wear the same thing—or worse—every day that you force me on the air.''

Stone's mouth widened into a maddeningly good-natured grin. ''Fine with me.''

She clenched her fists in her lap in an effort to control her anger, now at a full-pitch boil. ''If you don't believe me, just try me,'' she warned.

Stone nodded amiably, seemingly impervious to her icy tone. ''I believe you, Jamie. And like I said, that'll be just fine.''

Jamie opened her mouth, then closed it abruptly. He

sounded like he meant it. She stared at him, momentarily speechless.

Stone gave her another of his devastating grins, exposing the dimple that exactly matched the deep cleft in his chin. "Maybe you'd be interested in knowing what the folks of East Texas have to say about your new look." He reached behind him and punched the intercom button on the telephone. "Sue, would you please bring in the latest batch of phone messages?"

A moment later the secretary opened the office door. She cast a curious look at Jamie, handed a stack of pink notes to Stone and beat a hasty retreat.

Stone riffled through the papers. "Here's one. 'Liked the way that new girl looked today. Felt like I was getting the news from an old friend.'"

What? Jamie's brows drew together in confusion.

"Here's another one," Stone continued. "This one must be from a lady. 'It was great to see someone on TV at six in the morning who looks like I do at that hour.'" He looked up, his eyes twinkling, and chortled. "Boy, she must be a real mess." He returned his gaze to the message slips. "How about this—'I could focus on what that anchor was saying instead of being distracted by how she looked.'" Stone picked up the next message. "'Nice to see someone who looked like a real, flesh-and-blood person on TV.'"

Jamie's thoughts swam. People actually *liked* her sloppy look? It couldn't be. Stone was playing more mind games with her.

"Give me those," she said, leaning forward and reaching out a hand for the stack of messages. She was certain he'd been making up the remarks to goad her.

Stone grinned and relinquished the message slips. She cast him a challenging look before lowering her gaze to the small pink notes.

"'Finally there's a woman on TV who doesn't look like she's made out of plastic,'" she read. Stunned, Jamie glanced up at Stone who was leaning back on the desk, his arms straight, watching her. She drew out another message.

"'I could relate to that lady with the pigtails—I'd like to see more of her on the air.'" Jamie quickly flipped to another message and read, "'Where do I write to get an autographed photo of that new newsgirl?'"

Just because the flattering comments were written on message slips didn't mean they were authentic, Jamie thought. More than likely, it simply meant Stone had gone to more trouble than she'd first thought.

She dropped the messages in her lap and glared at Stone. "You must think I'm a real idiot if you expect me to fall for this reverse psychology plot."

Stone's mouth quirked into a grin. "Reverse psychology—is that what you think this is?"

Jamie sniffed haughtily. "I was born at night, but not last night. I know what you were up to yesterday with the consultant, and I know what you're up to now."

Stone rubbed his chin, his brows drawing together in a leathery furrow. "Let me see if I'm following this. I said I wanted you to have an everyday look, so you thought I really wanted you to have a dolled-up look." His eyes lit with amusement. "So you decided to go for a cleaning-out-the-garage look?"

Jamie gave one curt nod. "Exactly."

"And now you think these messages aren't real?"

Jamie nodded again.

"Well, if that doesn't beat all," Stone said softly, then reached for the phone. He pushed the speaker button, then one of the red blinking lights. "Good morning, KZZZ," he said, never taking his eyes from Jamie's face. "How may I help you?"

"I'm calling about that lady on the morning news," came a woman's voice.

"You must mean Jamie Erickson," Stone said, his eyes watching hers.

"That's right," replied the lady on the phone. "I just wanted to tell whoever is in charge of things that I think she's great. I normally watch channel four, but the TV was on your station when I turned it on this morning, and she looked so different I decided to watch for a while and, well, I thought she was terrific. So I just wanted to call and let someone know. Pass it along, will you?''

"I'll be happy to," Stone replied. "Thanks for calling."

A dial tone sounded, and Jamie glared at him defensively. "That could just be a fluke."

"Think so, huh?" Stone punched another line. "KZZZ."

"I loved that newslady this morning," a male voice crackled over the speakerphone. "I thought she made a profound political statement, going on the air dressed like that. She really made the point that the *issues* are what deserve our attention, not what people look like. All of us need to look beyond race and age and other surface differences and just *relate* to each other..."

"I appreciate your comments," Stone broke in just as the man seemed to be getting wound up, "and I'll pass them along. Thanks for calling."

He hung up the phone and looked at Jamie. Judging from her wide, shocked eyes, he'd finally gotten through to her. "Still think the phone messages were phony?"

"I guess not," she muttered. He watched her fingers move to the back of her neck and gently knead the muscles underneath her hair, and it struck him that her exposed nape was a highly sensual and immensely kissable spot.

"We can take some more calls, if you'd like."

She crumpled in the chair, a dazed look on her face. "No. I believe you."

Her defeated voice tugged at something in Stone's chest. "There are worse things than being a media darling, Jamie," he said gently. "Being an anchor has its compensations."

"Name one."

"Aside from the salary and the wardrobe allowance, you get invited to some great parties. Tonight, for example. The station is sponsoring a table at the Arts Ball. A lot of potential advertisers will be there and it's a great opportunity for the station to get some exposure."

"I hate big parties," Jamie protested. The Arts Ball was the biggest social event of the year. People came from five counties to attend the black-tie affair, which was held annually in the huge old mansion an oil millionaire had donated to the Fairfield Arts Council.

"We don't have to stay long. We'll put in an appearance and eat dinner, then we can leave."

"We?" Jamie shot him a questioning glance.

Stone nodded. "Mr. Milton asked me to take you. I'll pick you up at your house at seven."

"But I don't want..."

"Sorry, Jamie, but this is a command performance."

She twisted around in the chair to fully face him. "But I don't have anything to wear!"

Stone carefully kept his expression neutral. "Based on the response to what you wore this morning, maybe it's just as well. Might be a good idea to let that dowdy look be your signature."

She looked down at the baggy shirt and pulled it from her body. "You want me to go to the Arts Ball dressed like this?" she asked incredulously.

Stone shrugged, struggling to maintain a demeanor of indifference. If he showed the least bit of resistance, he was afraid she'd do just that. She'd been given a generous check to cover wardrobe expenses, and he could only hope she'd use some of it to buy something suitable for tonight's function. She was officially off duty after the noon broadcast today, so she'd have some time to shop.

He decided to give her an extra boost toward the mall. "Looking frumpy might be a good way to publicize our morning newscast."

He was gratified to see a stricken look crease the space between her eyes. She reached up and resumed rubbing her neck, her fingers massaging the very spot he'd decided earlier was begging for a kiss. A strong urge to bend down and plant one there seized him.

Stone took a step back. What was he thinking? He made a point to never hang around where he wasn't wanted, and it was clear that Jamie didn't want him. She'd already left him once. What was he waiting for—the graphics department to draw him a picture?

It had been a mistake for him to come back. It was over between them. He needed to accept it and move on. As far as Jamie was concerned, he wasn't just barking up the wrong tree, he was in the wrong forest.

He strode across the room and opened the door. Jamie rose and walked through it, holding herself stiffly erect. "I'll see you at seven," he said as he closed the door behind her.

If only, he thought ruefully, he could close his thoughts on Jamie as easily.

Chapter Five

The sky had deepened to a twilight haze when Stone pulled his white Jeep to a stop before the redbrick house at the edge of Fairfield's historic district. He studied the house through the windshield, taking in the high, peaked gables, the arched entryway, the long brick porch. The house was small, but distinctive. Just like Jamie.

The slam of his car door reverberated through the quiet neighborhood as he crossed the lawn and mounted the steps to her porch.

"Well, howdie-do," called a familiar voice. "Don't you look spiffy in your tuxedo!" He turned to see Grams rocking in a bench swing at the far end of the porch.

"You're looking pretty spiffy yourself, ma'am," he responded, walking toward her.

Grams beamed and adjusted the bow at the neck of her pink floral dress. She patted a spot on the swing beside her. "Have a seat. Jamie's still getting dressed."

"Does that mean she's wearing a dress?" Stone asked as he lowered himself onto the wooden seat.

Grams chortled. "You'll get to see for yourself in a moment. I think she wants to surprise you." Grams pushed her glasses up on the bridge of her nose. "I can't wait to see her myself. I stopped by to pick up a casserole dish and decided to stay and see the end result. It'll be better than anything on TV tonight."

No telling what *that* meant. For all he knew, Jamie was getting decked out like Boffo the Clown. He ran a hand down his face. "She sure surprised the heck out of me this morning. That granddaughter of yours is a real piece of work."

Grams looked up at him, her head cocked to one side like a bright-eyed bird. "Jamie doesn't like being told what to do. Never has. And she especially hates feeling manipulated."

Stone rubbed his chin. There was nothing he hated more, either. In fact, feeling manipulated by Jamie was one of things that had broken up their marriage. "Is that what she thinks I've been doing?"

"Well, isn't it?"

Stone sighed and pushed his foot against the wooden floor of the porch, setting the swing in motion. "I suppose. But why in blue blazes is she so dead set against doing something that's so clearly in her own best interests? Sometimes I don't understand her at all."

Grams patted his hand. "To understand Jamie, you need to understand her parents, and I know she's not very talkative on the topic. You only met Cheryl once, isn't that right?"

Cheryl was Jamie's mother. Stone nodded. "We flew down to Florida for a weekend visit right after we got married."

"Well, then, you probably noticed that my daughter is the flamboyant, outgoing type—the sort of gal who loves to be the center of attention. Her fondest dream was to be an actress and see her name in lights."

Stone rubbed his hand along the chain that suspended the swing from the overhang. The information fit his memory. He'd been surprised to discover that Jamie's mother had platinum hair, wore tons of jewelry and was given to sweeping, dramatic gestures. "She struck me as the exact opposite of Jamie."

Grams murmured her concurrence. "More to the point, Jamie is the exact opposite of her. Cheryl never made it to Broadway or Hollywood, and she desperately wanted her daughter to achieve the dream she never attained. She had too much time on her hands because that husband of hers was never around, so she put all of her energy into grooming Jamie for stardom."

Stone gazed at the old woman thoughtfully. "Let me guess. Jamie rebelled."

"Not at first. Jamie was an only child, anxious to please her mother, and eager to get her father's attention and approval. Her father was—" Grams hesitated, her mouth pursed "—I don't like to speak ill of the dead, but he was awfully critical. Anyway, Jamie wanted to make them proud of her, so she suffered through countless acting classes, dance recitals, singing lessons—you name it."

"And she hated it."

Grams nodded. "The ironic thing is Jamie was really good. By nature, she's always been on the quiet side, but she's got something that just kind of shines when she gets in front of an audience." Grams gave him a sideways look. "I guess she told you she used to stutter."

Stone nodded. "A friend of hers mentioned it, but Jamie never told me any details. She said she hates to talk about it. I brought it up a few times, but she'd always change the subject."

It was a technique Jamie employed on any topic she didn't want to discuss, Stone reflected—and it always made him feel shut out. Feeling like an outsider was a miserable, all-too-familiar sensation, one he'd experienced too often as a child. When Jamie clammed up, it brought back all those awful feelings. That same icy-cold fear would grip the pit of his stomach, that same emptiness would hollow out his chest, that same sawdust dryness would settle in his mouth. He hadn't known how to deal with that lonely, left-out feeling in his youth, and he hadn't figured it out in his marriage, either.

So he'd let her keep her distance. Sometimes he felt like there was a wall of glass between them—that he could see her, but never really touch her. Only in bed did he ever really feel that he'd broken through her wall of reserve.

He pulled his thoughts back to the topic at hand. "Jamie doesn't have any problem with stuttering now," he remarked.

"Not unless she's talking about it. The only time she stutters is when she discusses it, so she avoids the topic like the plague. After a long stretch of therapy, she's got it licked."

Stone's foot tensed, bringing the swing to an abrupt halt. Jamie's problem had been serious enough that she'd needed therapy? He'd been married to her for nearly a year. Why hadn't he known such a critical thing about her?

"How old was she when she started therapy?"

"She was in junior high. Her mother had pressured her into joining the speech club. In the middle of a debate in the school auditorium, she froze. She couldn't get the next word out. Oh, it was awful. She must have stuttered the same syllable over and over for a full couple of minutes. The kids started snickering, then outright laughing. Jamie ran off the stage in tears. And that was the end of her cooperation with her mother's plans. Jamie might be soft-spoken, but when she makes up her mind about something, she's as stubborn as a ox."

"I can vouch for that," Stone said softly. The images the old woman's words had conjured were vivid, and his heart ached with empathy. He knew all too well how painful ridicule could be.

"My guess is your pushing her to be an anchor reminds her of those early years, and she's not too happy about it." Grams reached over and patted his leg. "But don't feel like the Lone Ranger. She wasn't any too happy with me for arranging that little call-in, either."

Stone fingered the rough wood of the swing and gazed

at Grams thoughtfully. "So how do you recommend I handle things from here? I'm open to any and all suggestions."

Grams shook her head and shrugged her bony shoulders. "Afraid I don't have any answers for you. But I thought it might help if you understood the problem."

"What problem is that?" a familiar voice cut in.

Stone looked up to see a woman standing in the doorway, backlit by the hallway light. She wore something long and low and black, and it hugged every curve like a race car at the Indy.

Stone recognized the voice, but nothing else seemed the least bit familiar. He jumped to his feet. "Jamie?"

She stepped into the porch light, closing the door behind her. Stone couldn't keep from staring. His eyes traveled the length of her, taking in every detail from the shimmer of her rhinestone earrings to the tall, graceful heels of her satin shoes. He'd never seen her like this before—her hair pulled back in a sleek chignon, her eyes and lips outlined and colored, her body draped in a sophisticated number that accentuated every incredible inch.

"Jumpin' Jehoshaphat, Jamie," he breathed.

"I hope you aren't disappointed," Jamie said, lounging against the porch railing.

Stone's gaze riveted on her decolletage, mesmerized by the way it rose and fell with her every breath. "Disappointed?" he said vaguely, still trying to absorb the fact that this sophisticated creature was Jamie.

"That I'm not wearing a sweatshirt and pigtails."

Stone cleared his throat, trying to gather his wits about him. "N-no. No, not all."

"So what were you two talking about?"

"You mean...just now?" The moment the words were uttered, Stone realized he sounded like an idiot.

Jamie's eyebrow arched. "Yes, just now. You seemed to be discussing some kind of problem."

"Oh, that," Grams said, fluttering her hand in front of her face as though she were shooing away an invisible fly.

"I was just explaining the insect problem we have here in Fairfield. Such a nuisance!"

Jamie's expression clearly said she wasn't buying the story. "Yes, we do have a lot of pests." She aimed a pointed look at Stone. "And new ones migrate here every day."

Stone laughed. No matter how different she might look, this was still the same old Jamie. "Shall we go?"

"Do I have an option?"

Stone gave her a slow grin. Yep, same old Jamie, all right. The thought pleased him inordinately. "Not really. The station manager is dead set on having you attend this shindig."

Jamie couldn't suppress a laugh. "The ladies in charge of this ball would die of horror if they heard you refer to it as a shindig."

Stone held out his arm. "See? It's a good thing you're going with me to spare the station that embarrassment."

Jamie swallowed a bite of chocolate torte and nodded politely, feigning interest in the rambling chatter of Mrs. Milton, the station manager's wife. She was far too distracted by Stone's presence beside her at the linen-draped banquet table to pay much attention to the woman's prattle.

His nearness unnerved her. Stone, on the other hand, seemed oblivious to her. Throughout the elaborate five-course dinner, he'd been polite and cordial, addressing her just often enough to avoid the appearance of snubbing her, but paying no more attention to her than to the other eight people at the table.

True to his word, he wasn't doing anything that could possibly be construed as sexual harassment. In fact, he seemed to be going out of his way to keep his distance. She'd gotten far more attention from Todd, who'd unrelentingly glared at her across the table.

By all rights she should be relieved at Stone's business-like demeanor. So why did she feel so disappointed?

A white-gloved waiter began clearing the dishes. Across

the chandelier-studded ballroom, a dance band began to set up. Stone laid his napkin on the table, scooted back his chair and addressed the table at large. "I see a former colleague across the room. If you'll excuse me, I'll go say hello."

Jamie involuntarily tracked his progress across the room, noting that several other pairs of female eyes at neighboring tables did the same. It was no wonder, she admitted to herself. He was handsome as the devil in black-tie.

He stopped at a table on the far side of the room and touched the shoulder of a willowy blonde in a slinky red dress. The woman jumped to her feet, gave Stone a tight hug and kissed him on the cheek. Jamie watched the woman bat her eyes and smile at Stone seductively, standing far closer to him than necessary and giving him a good eyeful of her low-cut bodice.

Jamie's fingers tightened around the linen napkin in her lap, wadding it into a ball, as she glanced down at her own attire. Why had she gone to such pains tonight? She'd told herself she'd dressed in response to Stone's suggestion that she wear a sweatshirt, but she knew that was only an excuse.

The truth was she'd dressed to the nines out of plain old feminine pride. She'd wanted to prove she wasn't so average, so everyday, so run-of-the-mill after all. She'd dressed to impress him, and she might as well own up to it.

She knotted her napkin, as uncomfortable with the silent admission as she was with the fact it didn't seem to be working, and glanced back across the room. The blonde was fawning over him, her hand on his arm, her head thrown back in laughter.

Mrs. Milton leaned over conspiratorially. "Gordy tells me you used to be married to Stone. I don't know what happened, dear, but believe me, a girl could do a lot worse. He's positively adorable!"

Jamie stared at the gray-haired matron in surprise. Stone had told the station's manager that they used to be married?

Well, of course he would have, she realized. He'd always been aboveboard in his business dealings, and he would have wanted to be up-front about his relationship with the woman he was recommending as the new anchor. It would hurt his reputation to have the fact surface later. He could end up being accused of favoritism or nepotism or impropriety.

Impropriety. Hmm. Now there was a thought. Perhaps that was the ticket to getting off the air.

Jamie glanced back at Stone, just in time to see the blonde press a card into his hand.

No, she couldn't possibly. Could she?

"Does our former marriage pose a problem?" Jamie asked. "I remember reading something in the employee handbook about the station having a policy against romantic involvements between staff members, and it just occurred to me that your husband might object to ex-spouses working together."

Mrs. Milton's stiffly lacquered bouffant didn't budge as she shook her head and cast a glance at her husband across the table. "I've told Gordy that policy is the silliest rule he's ever come up with, but he won't listen to me. But don't worry, dearie." Mrs. Milton patted her hand. "That rule only applies to couples involved in an *active* romance, if you know what I mean."

The band struck up a slow forties' tune just as Stone returned to the table and lowered himself in his seat. The scent of a heavy, Oriental perfume clung to him, and a bright smear of lipstick colored his cheek. A flash of uncharacteristic jealousy ripped through Jamie. A touch of impropriety just might be in order after all.

She reached up and rubbed the smear from his face. He'd shaved this evening before picking her up, she thought distractedly as she touched him. Even so, his beard rasped her fingers ever so slightly, and the feel of it sent a shiver down her arm.

With an effort she pulled her hand away and gave him her brightest smile. "Let's dance," she urged.

Stone's eyes were guarded, his expression wary. Afraid he was about to refuse, she hopped out of her chair and tugged at his arm. "Come on. Don't be an old fuddy-duddy." She glanced to the side and was pleased to note that the entire table, including Mr. Milton, was watching with interest. She gave his arm another pull. "Come on—*honey*. This used to be one of our favorites."

He had no choice short of creating a scene. As he followed her to the dance floor, she smiled in satisfaction. The shoe's on the other foot now, she thought smugly.

As the music swelled, she turned toward him and placed her hand on his shoulder. He put his arm around her waist and swept her tight against him.

The moment he did, she realized she'd made an enormous mistake.

Oh, mercy. How could she have forgotten about this—how solid his chest felt, how perfectly her body fit against his, how muscular his thighs were as they nudged hers across the dance floor? The air contracted in her lungs and memories crowded out all other thoughts—memories of another night, of another ballroom, of the first time she'd danced with Stone.

It had been four years ago, at the TV station's Christmas party at a hotel in Tulsa. From the moment she'd stepped into his arms, she'd known she was a goner. Stone could have danced her through the city dump or to the moon and back and she never would have noticed. She'd been too wrapped up in the feel of him, the smell of him, the warmth of him—the sheer maleness of him.

She'd realized she was head over heels in love with him as they moved around the tinsel-strewn dance floor. They'd only been dating a few weeks, but she was certain he was the one. He was everything she'd ever dreamed of in a man—intelligent, funny, thoughtful, kind. And sexier than any man had a right to be.

But it was his intensity that attracted her most. He was a man who went after what he wanted, and he'd clearly wanted *her*. Being the focus of Stone's single-minded pursuit was the most thrilling thing she'd ever experienced.

As they'd danced together past the twinkling lights of a tall Christmas tree that night, he'd managed to thrill her further by whispering a soft question in her ear. Would she go skiing with him in Tahoe over Christmas?

She'd agreed in a heartbeat. She'd been at loose ends, anyway, that holiday season; Grams had signed up for a Christmas tour of the Holy Lands, and her mother had just remarried and moved to Florida. Although Jamie had been invited to join the newlyweds for the holidays, she'd felt reluctant to intrude.

So she'd gone with Stone to Tahoe—and ended up as a newlywed herself when their trip included a stop at a wedding chapel.

"Are you going to explain your sudden urge to dance, or should I just hazard a guess—*honey?*"

Jamie stiffened and pulled back, suddenly aware of her surroundings. She'd gotten caught up in the intoxicating feel of his long, hard length pressed against her, his clean, familiar scent, his hand resting low on the small of her back. She'd completely lost sight of the reason why she'd asked Stone to dance in the first place.

She glanced around and noticed he'd maneuvered them to the far side of the dance floor, away from the KZZZ table. Other dancers obscured them from the view of the very people she was hoping to shock.

Oh, dear. This wasn't working—not at all. Jamie looked up at Stone's face and was rattled to find his lips curved in wry amusement.

"Let me take a stab at it. You want Mr. Milton to think we're involved. Am I right?"

Jamie diverted her gaze away from his face and stared unseeingly at the other dancers. The heat from his gaze warmed her face, and she had the uncomfortable sensation he could see right through her.

"And let me guess the reason. You want him to think

I'm violating the station's policy prohibiting personnel in the same department from dating.''

She'd be damned if she'd give him the satisfaction of a response. She continued to look away, her lips clenched tightly together.

He cupped a hand under her chin and tilted her face upward, giving her no choice but to look in his walnut eyes. "It won't work, Jamie. In the first place, I'm a consultant, not an employee, so the rule doesn't apply. In the second place, if you're trying to create the impression that you were placed on the air because of our relationship instead of your merits, you're way off track. The audience response to you is too strong—and audience response is the only thing Mr. Milton cares about."

He released her chin, reclaimed his hold on her back and guided her in a smooth spin. "I just wish I could say the same, Jamie," he murmured into her hair.

Jamie's heart thudded in her chest. "What do you mean?"

Stone pulled back enough to look down into her eyes. "I mean it's been a long time since I've felt anything as good as you feel right now in my arms."

The words chased through her, warming her like a hot toddy on an icy day. "How long?" she whispered.

"Three years, two months and—" he paused for a moment and counted under his breath "—twelve days."

The words shattered what few remnants of her composure remained. If he hadn't been holding her, she was sure her legs would have buckled.

"I told you I wouldn't touch you unless you made the first move," Stone murmured in her hair. "It seems to me you made it when you asked me to dance."

She searched her mind for a response and found that all coherent thought had fled. Emotion, strong and thick as his shoulder muscles under her hand, clutched her throat as Stone pulled her close and spun her around. She clung to him and danced. The room, the people in it, the very music itself seemed to recede into the distance. The world narrowed to just the moment, to just Stone and the sensations he stirred at every point of contact—the rasp of his clean-shaven beard against her cheek, the warm weight of his hand above her buttocks, the solid pressure of his thigh against hers.

All too soon, from what seemed to be a great distance, she became aware that the song had ended. She wobbled on her high heels as she stepped back from him, and he clutched her arms to steady her.

"Thanks for the dance, Jamie." His breath was warm on her face but she didn't dare look up to meet his gaze. She was too unsure of what she might read in his eyes or what he might see in hers.

She was excruciatingly aware of his hand on her elbow as he escorted her back to the table. She was all jangled nerves and raw emotions, and she knew she couldn't possibly sit back down and resume a round of small talk with the other people at the table. She needed a few moments to collect herself. Murmuring an excuse, she grabbed her purse and fled to the ladies' room.

Inside the brightly lit lounge, Jamie dampened a paper towel, pressed it to her neck and drew a deep breath.

"It's hot out there on the dance floor," commented a middle-aged woman washing her hands at the next sink.

Hotter than you'd ever imagine. Jamie gave a weak smile and was relieved when the woman dried her hands and left.

Exhaling harshly, Jamie ran the cool towel across her throat, where her pulse raced at a fevered pace. She needed to get a grip on herself; she was overreacting, plain and simple. Stone had done nothing more than admit he'd missed her. She was making too much out of the fact that he'd kept track of the exact number of days they'd been apart. The chemistry between them had always been volatile, and that, no doubt, was what he'd been referring to.

And it was the reason she was responding this way, she rationalized. The only thing that remained between them was physical attraction, and she needed to take care not to make it into something it was not. After all, chemistry didn't make a marriage. It wasn't even enough to save one.

Marriage took two people willing to share their lives, two people working toward the same goals. Stone had spent most of their marriage at work, pursuing his own agenda. He didn't have room in his life for a wife. He was wedded to his career, and she'd do well to keep the fact in mind. Jamie tossed the paper towel in the trash as she left the rest room, thinking she needed to do the same thing with her romantic illusions.

A cold hand grabbed her elbow as she entered the dimly lit ballroom on her way back to the table. Startled, she looked up and found herself gazing into Todd's bloodshot eyes.

"I understand you and that fancy-schmancy consultant used to be married." His tongue was thick, his words slurred. "Did getting you that anchor gig reduce his alimony payments?"

"I don't get any alimony from Stone." Jamie tried to pull free of his grasp, but Todd's fingers dug deeper into her arm.

"No? Then I guess there's some other type of compensation involved." Todd bared his teeth in a lecherous grin. "You two sure looked cozy on the dance floor."

Dancing with Stone had been an even bigger mistake than she'd realized. Still, how dare Todd make such a crude insinuation? Jamie fought to keep her temper in check. "You've had too much to drink, Todd. You should go home before you embarrass yourself. Do you want me to call you a cab?"

His lips curled in a sneer. "Don't worry about me, little lady. You've got plenty to worry about just looking out for yourself."

A shiver shimmied up her spine. She yanked her arm free, turned on her heel and scurried across the ballroom.

Her knees were weak when she sank into her chair and her hand shook as she reached for her water glass.

Stone studied her trembling hand, then turned his dark

eyes on her face, his gaze searching. "Are you all right, Jamie?"

She hesitated, hating to tattle on Todd despite his unnerving behavior. After all, she *had* taken the man's job and gotten him demoted, even if it wasn't her choice or design. The man was drunk, that was all, and if she said anything to Stone, he'd make certain Todd got fired. "I'm fine," she said. "It's just a little stuffy in here, that's all."

"I promised you we didn't have to stay late. Are you ready to leave?"

Relief poured through her at the suggestion. "Yes. It's been a long day."

They said their goodbyes and were nearing the ballroom exit when a flash went off in Jamie's face.

She stopped and blinked. When she quit seeing stars, she realized she was staring at a tall, wiry man wielding a camera. He gave a gap-toothed smile. "I'm with the morning newspaper, Ms. Erickson. Can I get another shot of you?"

Stone quickly stepped aside. Before Jamie could frame a protest, the flash blinded her again.

"Thanks, Ms. Erickson," the man said, lowering his camera. Stone took her by the elbow and steered her toward the exit.

"What was that all about?" Jamie asked.

Stone grinned down at her. "Your new celebrity status."

"I felt like the victim of an ambush."

"I'm afraid it goes with the territory." He looked down at her as they crossed the brightly lit foyer to the exit. "But you have nothing to worry about, Jamie. You couldn't take a bad picture if you tried." He held the door open for her.

It wasn't the outcome of the picture that bothered her; it was the fact she was an object of attention. She'd avoided the spotlight ever since that disastrous episode in junior high, and she didn't like finding herself unwillingly thrust back into it. It gave her a cold, queasy feeling, as if she were walking a tightrope and it were only a matter of time before she fell off.

She shivered, as much from the thought as the chilly

night air. Stone immediately shrugged off his jacket and held it out for her. She hesitated a moment, then let him slip it on her.

The lining held the rich warmth of his body heat, and the intimacy of it sent a shimmy of pleasure dancing through her. It reminded her of the way he used to warm the sheets on her side of the bed.

The memory made her heart trip—and when he gave her a rakish grin and put his arm around her, it quickened into double time. "Still have that Southern Belle blood, I see. I'll bet your feet are freezing."

His gaze fell to her open-toed satin slippers. Her cold feet had been a running joke between them, and the mention of it now made her stomach constrict.

"Do you still sleep in wool socks?"

She used to sleep in socks and nothing else. A rush of heat flooded her face, and she was glad the parking lot was dimly lit. "What I sleep in is none of your business."

"I remember when it used to be." And I'd like to make it my business again, he silently added, opening the Jeep door for her.

The sudden clarity of the thought startled him. He'd come to Fairfield unsure of what he wanted from her, not knowing what he hoped would happen. Hell, he still didn't know. He only knew what he hoped would happen tonight.

He rounded the vehicle and climbed in. After the noise and bustle of the ballroom, the vehicle seemed as secluded as a desert island.

He watched her wrap his jacket tightly across her chest, hiding her decolletage from view. Lucky jacket, he thought wryly. It got to caress her skin, to touch the shadows between her breasts that had enchanted him all evening, to snuggle up against her smooth, creamy skin.

"A lot of things are different now," she retorted.

He stretched his arm across the back of the seat, his hand a scant inch from her head. He longed to loosen the pins holding her hair in that upswept arrangement and twirl the golden strands around his fingers. He could practically feel the silken texture sliding through his hands, practically smell the faint, rich aroma her loose hair always had, a scent lighter than perfumes or shampoo, a scent that was purely her. "Do you ever wish they weren't, Jamie?"

Her eyes closed for longer than a blink. When she opened them, she looked away. He wondered if she would lie. He wondered if he'd be able to tell if she did.

"I don't think that's something we should be discussing."

Ah, avoidance. A tougher nut to crack than deception. He'd have to try new tactic.

He started the Jeep engine, turned on the heat and pulled out of the parking lot. "What would you like to talk about?"

He felt the warmth of her gaze on his face. "What have you being doing for the past three years?"

Missing you. He choked back the words and slanted a glance at her as he steered the car onto the thoroughfare. "Working. First at the Seattle station, then Denver and Baltimore. I started my company last year, and I've been all over the map ever since. In a different market every two months."

He glanced again at her profile. He'd always been moved by the sight of her from this angle, had always found the ever-so-slight tilt of her nose, the sweep of her lashes, the curve of her chin to be somehow heartbreaking. Her profile wasn't classic, but it was nevertheless exquisite, as beautiful as a cameo. It occurred to him that he'd never told her that, never told her how the sight of it softened something inside him, like the sun on an icy pond.

It was one of many things he'd never told her. There were evidently a lot of things she'd never told him, either, he thought, his mind flashing to his earlier conversation with Grams. For a couple of people in the communications industry, they'd sure done a damn poor job of it.

If he'd been more open, if *she'd* been more open, where would they be now? Still together, going home to share a double bed?

The thought made his chest ache. Maybe he should say something. Maybe he should tell her he'd missed her, or mention how her profile affected him, or just say how good she'd felt when they'd danced together.

He started to speak, but the rigid way she held her head froze the words on his tongue.

He'd learned about rejection early in life, and the lesson he'd learned best was to avoid it whenever he could. Jamie had rejected him once; what made him think things would be any different now?

He pulled his eyes back to the road, swallowed around the cold lump in his throat and forced a levity he didn't feel into his voice. "How about you? Have you done much traveling?"

"No. While you were on the road, I've been busy putting down roots."

There it was again—that old accusatory edge in her voice, that familiar defensive tone. A ripple of old pain flowed through him. He'd wanted so badly to make her proud of him, but she'd been too busy resenting the amount of time he devoted to his career to see any merit to his work. Why couldn't she have understood he'd needed to dedicate himself to his career to get it off the ground? She should have been glad he had some drive and ambition, should have been proud of his achievements. What did she want—a lazy, no-good drifter like his father?

A deeper wave of pain washed over him as old memories surged in. His mother, always tired and haggard, working two jobs to support him and his father. His father, raiding his mother's purse to finance his gambling habit; cold, dark nights without electricity because his father had detoured to the racetrack on his way to pay the light bill. The taunts of schoolmates when his dad was jailed after another barroom brawl—*Dumb Bum Johnson's dad's in jail. Too lazy to work and he can't make bail.*

Stone's fingers ached and he realized he was gripping the steering wheel so hard his knuckles had turned white.

He relaxed his hands and pulled one up to rake through his hair, trying to banish the memories from his mind.

The truth about his father was another thing he'd never told Jamie. She knew his family had been far from wealthy, but she had no idea how bad things had been or how ashamed he'd felt. He'd often wanted to tell her, but he'd never known how. He'd spent so many years covering up his childhood that it seemed impossible to initiate a discussion about it.

Especially since Jamie's own background was the exact opposite of his own. Her father had been a successful, high-ranking executive with a Fortune 500 company, a pillar of the community. She'd grown up with money and security and most importantly, a sense of respectability.

There was no way she could understand. Oh, she knew about getting along without much money—he'd been impressed with the fact she'd been living frugally when he'd met her, supporting herself on her own tightly budgeted salary—but she had no frame of reference to the bone-crushing neglect and poverty he'd known as a child. There was no way she could really comprehend it, and the last thing he wanted from her was pity.

Besides, what did it matter, anyway? The old man had been dead for years, and his mother had died two years before he'd met Jamie. The only thing that mattered now was that he was making good on his vow to be the exact opposite of his deadbeat dad.

Stone turned the car onto Jamie's street. He hadn't meant to let the whole trip pass in silence. He had an aching need to try to set things right between them, to somehow jump over the wall they'd built.

He glanced at her as he pulled up before her home. "Tell me about your house. How long have you had it?"

Her face looked as though a light switch had been flipped on. He'd definitely hit on the right topic, he noted with satisfaction.

"I bought it last year. It was a HUD house—a repo—

and I got it at an auction for a steal. It needs a lot of work, but I fell in love with it—and love fixing it up.''

She'd always wanted a home. He remembered that she used to keep a folder filled with photos and magazine clippings—her dream file, she called it, full of decorating ideas.

Stone peered through the dark at the structure, illuminated by a light on the porch. "It reminds me of a gingerbread house.''

"It's the way the mortar spills out between the bricks. It's called weeping brick. It's a technique that was used in the thirties and forties.''

"Did you do the landscaping?''

"Yes.'' Her voice filled with pride. "The trees were already there, but I put in the shrubbery and flower beds. This year I'm going to start a vegetable garden in the backyard, too.''

"I'm impressed. What about the inside?''

"It's still a work in progress. So far I've refinished the hardwood floors and redone all the paper and paint.''

"I'd love to see it.''

She hesitated a moment, then smiled. "Come on. I'll give you the grand tour.''

Stone smiled as he rounded the car to open her door. Yes indeedy, talking about the house was definitely a wise move.

"One of the changes I want to make when I can afford it is to get a beveled glass front door,'' she said as they approached the porch.

He stood behind her as she fumbled in her purse for her key and looked at the nape of her neck, longing to plant a kiss on it, his mind far removed from front doors. He bent his head to see if he could smell her perfume and was rewarded with a soft, intoxicating scent. He closed his eyes, craned his head forward and inhaled appreciatively. When he opened them, Jamie stood in the open doorway, regarding him curiously.

Realizing he looked ridiculous, he feigned a sneeze.

"Bless you!" Her brow crinkled into concern. "I shouldn't have taken your jacket. You're catching cold."

The worried look on her face tugged at something in his chest, something he'd thought long-dead and buried. She shrugged out of the tuxedo coat and held it out to him. He had no choice but to take it, although he was strangely reluctant to do so. He liked the idea of something of his wrapping around her, touching her skin, keeping her warm.

"Would you like some hot tea—or coffee?"

He was certain she made the offer purely for medicinal reasons, but what the heck. He wasn't going to pass up an opportunity to extend his stay. He draped the jacket over his arm and smiled. "Coffee sounds great."

She crossed the room, switched on a lamp and looked at him expectantly. With a start, he remembered that he was ostensibly here to see the house. He pulled his gaze away from her to look around the room.

His eyebrows flew up in amazement. It looked like something out of a magazine. Though not in a fussy, museumy, don't-sit-on-the-furniture sort of way, he thought, as his gaze traveled from the small brick fireplace in the corner to the stitched samplers on the wall. Nothing really matched, but the overall effect was stunning. The room was filled with warm colors and mixed prints and had the home-spun ambience of a farmhouse or country inn.

"This is terrific! You did all this on a producer's salary?"

She nodded. "I tried to make up in creativity what I lacked in funds. The two armchairs came from a flea market. I reupholstered them myself."

Was that the sofa she'd bought when they were married, covered in a different fabric? It had been a sore spot then, and seeing it now hurt like an old wound.

He hadn't wanted to acquire any furniture, much less real estate. Relocation was the name of the game in TV news management, and he'd wanted to be unencumbered, free to climb the next rung of the career ladder on a moment's notice. He'd argued that it was easier to rent an apartment along with furnishings and appliances than to hassle with packing, unpacking and moving.

But she'd longed for a home, for roots. They'd had a terrible argument when she'd bought the sofa. Not about the sofa, exactly. The real issue had been the long hours and the frequent moves and the lack of stability created by his career. He'd told her he was trying to create a secure future for them and that she wasn't being supportive. She'd said he would never be satisfied, that no point in his career would ever be enough, that he would always be living in the future instead of in the present.

A raw, hungry feeling gnawed at his gut as he looked around. It looked like she was managing to make her dreams come true just fine without him. The room was beautiful, as warm and inviting as Jamie herself, filled with baskets and plants and other items that looked like they'd been collected and cared for over time.

He thought of his sterile hotel room and hated the thought of going back to it tonight.

She placed her purse on a side table. "I'll get the coffee started."

He followed her into a tiny kitchen, painted the rusty red of an old barn. A collection of whimsical chicken prints covered one wall and a ceramic rooster stood guard on a small oak table in the narrow breakfast nook. It was inviting and homey and warm, and he wondered what it would be like to sit at that table in the mornings and sip coffee across from Jamie.

She filled the coffeepot with water and pulled a paper filter out of cabinet. He went to the freezer to get the coffee, remembering she always kept it there because she thought it stayed fresher. Despite the domesticity her house radiated, he noticed that the freezer was stocked with TV dinners.

He stared at the frosty pile of boxes, memories swirling around him like the cloud of frozen air. Cooking had been a hobby they'd shared when they'd first gotten married. They'd loved surprising each other with gastronomic experiments, and shopping together had been an adventure. Finding a perfect fillet, an unusual herb or an exotic fruit had been a cause for celebration.

Good God, what had happened? They'd moved to Phoenix and he'd started working practically around the clock, that was what happened, he thought with a wince. He'd barely had time for sleep, much less meals or hobbies.

Or Jamie.

A sudden sense of grief stabbed him. Their marriage had once been bright, joy-filled, packed with love. How could they have let it die?

He handed her the coffee, then held up a box of frozen lasagna. "Not cooking much these days?"

She glanced up, and a stricken look passed over her face, and he knew she, too, remembered. Turning away, she unfolded the bag of coffee. "No." She poured a scoopful of grounds into the coffee maker. "How about you?"

"I keep an apartment in Seattle, but I live in hotel rooms. Standing in your kitchen right now is the closest I've come to a culinary experience in months."

Jamie pressed a button on the coffee maker and turned toward him, her smile overly bright. "I guess people like us keep the frozen food companies in business. Come on. I'll show you the rest of the house while the coffee brews."

He followed her down a hallway, peering into rooms along the way—a guest bedroom, a room she used as an office and a guest bath.

"And this is my bedroom." She flipped on a switch, and he stepped inside. The tightness that had constricted his chest all evening threatened to squeeze the air from his lungs.

The room looked like Jamie, smelled like Jamie, felt like Jamie—soft and rosy and warm. She'd always loved quilts, and the room reflected the fact. A quilt in an elaborate star pattern hung on the wall, and another one in similar shades of green and rose and blue covered an old four-poster bed. Still another quilt lay folded at the foot of the bed—one she no doubt used for extra warmth on her feet at night. A rocking chair in the corner sported a quilt cushion and throw pillow.

But the thing that stabbed his heart like a knife was the wooden music box on her bureau. He crossed the room and picked it up, lifting the lid. A tiny bride and groom turned on a pedestal as the familiar strains of "We've Only Just Begun" filled the air.

A knot rose in his throat. He'd bought the music box for her at the wedding chapel where they'd been married. They'd laughed about how corny, how sappy, how touristy the souvenir was, but throughout their marriage, Jamie had displayed it in a place of honor.

He looked at her, his eyes questioning.

"You kept this."

Jamie's heart slammed against her chest. Why, oh why, had she left that blasted thing out in plain view? She attempted to shrug, wanting to diminish the significance of his discovery, but the gesture ended in a shiver. She felt exposed, laid bare, emotionally naked. Why had she let Stone into her house? It was like letting him back into her life, into her heart.

Into *her*. The thought made her shiver again.

Still holding the box, he stepped toward her until he was so close she could smell the woodsy scent of his cologne. The tiny twirling figures were spinning more slowly now, the musical notes dragging through the air.

"Why did you keep this, Jamie?" he asked again.

She shrugged, avoiding his eyes. He set the box on the chest of drawers behind him and reached for her, his hands on the backs of her arms.

"What happened to us?" His voice was low and ragged. When she looked up, his eyes were as dark and troubled as the bottom of a muddy river.

Her heart tore all over again, ripping along the old frazzled seam. Three years of mending, of trying to knit together a life without Stone, were unraveled by a few words. Three years of pretending she was all right, of telling herself she was over him, of acting as if it didn't matter, were suddenly exposed as being nothing but pure fabrication, woven of the same cloth as the emperor's new clothes.

Well, she'd be damned if she'd let him know it. She straightened her back and lifted her chin. "You left, that's what happened."

"I wanted you to come with me."

"I was sick to death of moving! My entire childhood was one move after another, and I didn't want the rest of my life to be like that, too. Besides, I'd just been awarded a grant to produce that documentary."

"I didn't know about your grant when I accepted the job."

"That's the point. I'd become such a small part of your life that you accepted the job without consulting me. You just assumed I'd pick up and move with you, like I had all the times before."

"You were never a small part of my life, Jamie." His voice was adamant, his eyes intense. His fingers tightened on her arm. "I wanted to discuss it with you, but I had to give an answer right away, and you were out in the boonies producing that feature about the children's camp. The job was too good to pass up." He looked at her long and hard, then dropped his hands and exhaled harshly. "I thought you trusted me to make the right decision. I was trying to build a solid career so we could have a good future, Jamie. You knew when you married me that my career would require a lot of relocation for a few years."

"I didn't know that every time we moved I'd see less and less of you. You were putting in such long hours I don't see how you could tell if we were even in the same town or not."

He drew a deep breath. "It was just temporary. I didn't intend to keep that kind of work schedule forever."

She threw back her head and glared at him. "Neither did my father. It was always just one more promotion, just one more move—but it was never enough. Every success he obtained just made him want another, until there was no time in his life for anything else. There ought to be a support group for people like you—Success Junkies Anonymous.''

The music box ground to a halt. Silence hung in the air, heavy as a wet blanket.

He reached out and touched her again, this time cupping his hand around her head, his thumb tracing a line down her cheek. When he spoke, his voice was a low, raw whisper. "I'm sorry, Jamie. I didn't realize how I was hurting you.''

Her heart twisted. The last thing she'd expected was an apology. Stone always had a reason for every action, a rebuttal to every argument.

Well, it was too late. He should have thought of apologizing three years ago. "I told you that if you left, our marriage was over. You left anyway.''

"You issued an ultimatum. You were trying to manipulate me.''

Their gazes clashed like lightning, filling the room with an electric charge.

He was right. She'd been bluffing, trying to make him turn down the job. She should have known it wouldn't work. Nothing got his back up faster than someone trying to pull one over on him. Her ploy had not only backfired, it had blown up in her face.

"I never thought you'd really leave," she whispered.

The corners of his eyes feathered with pain. "I never thought you'd stay behind.''

The silence thundered between them as their eyes locked and held. "Stone," she finally breathed.

"Ja—" His mouth was on hers before he'd finished her name. He pulled her to him, one arm around her back, one hand in her hair and claimed her lips possessively.

It felt like coming home. Nothing had ever felt as good, as right as Stone's arms, Stone's mouth, Stone's body pressed against hers. There was nothing tentative about his kiss. It was flat-out, full throttle, pedal to the metal. He pulled her closer, flattening her breasts against his hard chest, and suckled her bottom lip, drawing it into his mouth.

Oh, mercy, how she'd missed him—missed *this.* His tongue plundered her mouth as she clung to him, giving as good as she got. Her hands worked down the muscled cords of his neck to the taut sinew of his back, reveling in the familiar, thrilling feel of him. His skin burned through his starched cotton shirt.

He unzipped her dress and reached inside, his fingers traveling upward to nudge the fabric off her shoulders. The dress spilled off her, puddling at her feet.

His gaze spread over her like butter on warm bread, making her glad she'd worn a garter belt and stockings. He gave a throaty sigh. "Ah, Jamie, you're so beautiful."

He made her feel that way. She arched her back as he unfastened her black lace bra and cupped her breasts, lowering his head to draw a dusky tip into his mouth. She moaned and dug her fingers into the springy waves of his hair, bending forward to kiss the top of his head.

He lavished attention on the other breast, then nibbled his way up her neck to reclaim her mouth. She moaned and moved her hips against him, and he slid his hands down to cup her bottom.

His desire fed hers. She was inflamed, on fire, ablaze. She curled a leg around his thigh, teetering on one high heel.

He groaned, shifted his hands lower and lifted her off her feet. His mouth still on hers, he carried her to the bed.

Jamie was only vaguely aware of the mattress beneath her. The far more urgent sensation of Stone kneeling astride her, his lips trailing down her breasts, claimed all of her attention. She was drowning in passion, awash in desire for this man she'd loved and married.

Loved, married—and divorced.

What on earth was she doing? She'd spent the last three years trying to get over her ex-husband, and here she was, about to make love with him. The realization struck her like a splash of cold water.

"Stone," she murmured. "Stone—we can't."

He raised his head from her breast. "If you need protection, honey, I'll go to the store…"

"It's not that. It's…it's…Stone, we've got to talk. Stone—are you listening?"

He sighed heavily as he sat up, dragging a hand through his hair. "You've got my full attention, Jamie."

She clutched a pillow to her chest and scooted up against the headboard. "Making love won't solve anything."

He swung his legs off the edge of the bed and stood to adjust his slacks, which pulled tight across a distinctive bulge. "I can think of one thing it would solve pretty well."

"You know what I mean, Stone. I can't just have a fling with you."

"Is that what you think we're doing?"

"I don't know what we're doing. It's all happening too fast." She pulled up higher against the headboard, reaching for another pillow. "You'll be gone in two months. If anything your life is more transient now than it as when we were married."

"Jamie, honey—I won't have this life-style forever."

"When will you settle down? In a year?"

He rubbed a hand through his hair. "I don't know, Jamie."

"Five years?"

"I just said I don't know."

"Ten?"

His silence told her all she needed to know. "Nothing's changed, Stone. We're right where we were when you walked out the door and ended our marriage."

"No, we're not," he said softly.

"What's different now?"

He gazed at her a long moment, taking in her tousled hair, her kiss-swollen lips, her enormous eyes. Something inside of him flared to life, like a match to a pilot light in a long-vacant house. "I am. *I'm* different, Jamie."

And in that moment he knew he was. Not just because he was older and wiser, but because he now knew what it was like to live without her. She'd left a void in his heart that was Jamie-sized and Jamie-shaped, a void that no one else could ever fill.

He wanted back in her life. He didn't know for how long or on what terms, and right now he didn't even care. He was like a deep-sea diver who'd surfaced too quickly. He needed to decompress, and the only way to do that was to resubmerge himself in a relationship with her, fast and deep.

He wanted her back. He wanted to make love to her until they were sated and exhausted and weak as kittens. He wanted to hold her as she slept, to wake with her in his arms, to make love to her all over again in the morning.

But judging from the guarded expression on her face, it wasn't going to happen tonight.

He stretched out his hand to touch her, then stopped himself. If he touched her again, it would just make it harder to leave.

He drew a harsh breath. "It's late, and you have an early morning. I'll let you get some sleep. I'll see you at the station tomorrow." It was time to go, but his feet felt like lead. He couldn't leave without extracting some small concession, some tiny basis for hope. "I'd like to take you to dinner Friday."

"I don't think seeing each other outside of work is a good idea."

He gave his most persuasive smile. "Come on, Jamie. The frozen food company won't miss your business for one night. You're not afraid, are you?"

It was a shamelessly cheap shot. He knew she hated admitting she was afraid of anything.

Right now she looked scared to death.

"Of course not," she retorted.

He grinned at the way he'd called that one. "Well, then, it's a date."

"But I can't," she protested. "I'm signed up for a gardening seminar. It starts Friday evening and runs all weekend."

He wasn't going to let her off that easily. "So we'll make it Monday." His gaze trailed down her body and snagged at the top of her garter-belted thigh. He drew a rough breath. "See you at the station tomorrow, Jamie."

He hustled himself out of her house as quickly as possible, welcoming the chill night air. He hoped the hotel had plenty of cold water; it was going to take a long, icy shower to bring his body temperature back down to anywhere near normal.

Chapter Six

Jamie folded her hands on top of the anchor desk and stared blankly at the monitor, ignoring the commercial on the screen, as last night's encounter with Stone replayed in her mind.

In the cold light of morning, she couldn't believe how close she'd come to letting herself get carried away. Stone's lips had felt so delicious, his arms around her so strong and right, his body so firm and masculine and *ready....*

But it was the emotion between them that had nearly been her undoing. Had the end of their marriage really been as painful for him as it had been for her? She'd never thought so; he'd walked away too easily. When she'd issued that ultimatum, he hadn't argued, hadn't begged, hadn't bargained. He'd simply gone.

But last night she'd seen something in his eyes she'd never seen before, something dark and deep and sad, and his voice had been gruff with pain when he asked her what had happened to their marriage. And she'd been stunned to discover he knew to the day exactly how long they'd been apart. Last night he hadn't acted like a man who'd shrugged off his marriage lightly.

Had she been wrong to think he'd never really been in love with her? During the past three years, she'd told herself he'd never loved her as she'd loved him, repeating it like a mantra to keep away a more painful thought—that he'd buried himself in his work to avoid her, because he'd discovered some deep, unlovable flaw in her.

Stone had always been hard to read. He said he'd changed. Had he really? And if so, how?

She'd spent the night tossing and turning and weighing the possibilities, her heart fluttering wildly with hope, her emotions vacillating between joy and despair until she thought she'd lose her mind.

This morning, though, she'd forced herself to look squarely at the facts, and the most significant fact was that Stone had been unable to answer her questions about his career plans. He evidently hadn't changed at all, at least not in the way that mattered, and if she got involved with him again, she'd be right back where she started. She was only borrowing trouble by fantasizing that things could be different.

The director's voice boomed over the intercom. "We're coming out of the break. Standby. Ten, nine..." Jamie blinked and stared at the page in front of her. It wasn't like her to lose her concentration during a newscast. But then, it wasn't like her to stay up all night, either, aroused and disturbed and confused.

Unless she wanted to run the risk of stuttering on the air, she'd better focus her attention on the task in front on her. She drew a deep breath, centered her thoughts on the next story and pasted a smile on her face as the camera light blinked on.

Twenty minutes later she heaved a sigh of relief and unfastened the microphone from her lapel. She still hated being on the air, but the brutal terror that had gripped her the first few times had loosened its hold a bit. Stone's confidence in her abilities seemed to be contagious and she was beginning to have some faith in her ability to make it through a newscast without stuttering.

Harold shut off the set lights, plunging the studio back into dimness. When Jamie's eyes adjusted, she saw Stone leaning against the wall. Thoughts of the night before sent her pulse rate soaring. *Nothing's changed,* she told herself sternly, but her heart fast danced anyway. She rose from her seat as he walked toward her.

"Good morning." His straight, white teeth flashed in a smile. "Did you sleep well?"

"Great," she lied. "And you?"

"Nary a wink."

His low, sexy tone sent a shiver of attraction chasing through her. With an effort she pulled herself erect. "I think we need to forget about last night and focus on work."

"There's no way I'm likely to forget anything about you, Jamie, but we can talk about work if you like." He grinned as his eyes ran over her tailored red suit. "You did a nice job this morning. But what happened to the sweat suit and pigtails?"

Jamie lifted her shoulders. If she had to be in front of the public, she might as well have some dignity about her while she did it.

"Not that I have any complaints," Stone continued. "After all, you're the new chameleon of fashion, so you can wear whatever you damn well please."

"What are you talking about?"

"This morning's paper." He handed her the front page of the life-styles section. A picture of her at last night's function ran next to a fuzzier image of her in pigtails with a caption underneath explaining the photo was from yesterday's newscast.

Her eyes scanned the story, which was written in the flowery style of the paper's gossip columnist. "KZZZ's new anchorwoman has the whole county buzzing. In addition to delivering the news with heretofore-unheard-of empathy and emotion, she refuses to conform to standard dress-for-success rules. Her unorthodox casual look takes the anchor desk off a pedestal and places it in the living room with the viewers."

"Oh, brother," she muttered. She glanced farther down the article. "By contrast, her glamorous new look at last night's Arts Ball proves she's refreshingly unafraid to reveal a sexy, feminine side. Ms. Erickson is shaping up as a true chameleon of fashion, a brave trailblazer bold enough to be a genuine role model for today's multidimensional woman."

Jamie looked up at Stone and made a face. "A person needs hip boots to wade through this article!"

"I especially like the last line," Stone remarked.

"'We can hardly wait to see what she does next,'" Jamie read aloud.

The laugh lines at the edge of Stone's eyes deepened as he smiled. "Neither can I, Jamie. I've got to hand it to you, you've gotten more PR for this station in two days than I've been able to achieve most places in six months. You've got half the state tuning in just to see what you'll look like next."

"Great, just great."

"From the station's standpoint, it is." His brown eyes searched her face. "I wish you could be as happy about this as Mr. Milton is. Are you ready to level with me about why you're bucking this promotion like a bull with a pair of spurs in his side?"

She gazed up at him and bit her bottom lip, tempted to blurt out everything. But another part, the silent gatekeeper within, refused to allow it. That part never let anyone, not even Stone, get too close.

The high, protective wall had been there since early childhood and had grown taller and thicker each time her father had belittled her. She'd grown up believing she was flawed and unacceptable. He'd drilled it into to her that her only chance of succeeding in life lay in pretending to be strong and confident, in concealing any and all weaknesses.

She no longer subscribed to her father's belief intellectually, but how she felt about it emotionally was an altogether different matter. And it hadn't helped that Stone had told her early in their courtship that two of the things he loved most about her were her strength and independence.

She'd never completely let down her guard, not even in their marriage, and she wasn't about to start now. The last thing she needed was to make herself more vulnerable to Stone than she already was.

She straightened her back and lifted her head. "I don't like being forced to do things I don't want to do, that's all."

Stone gave a rueful smile, his eyes tinged with something that looked like regret, as though he were disappointed that she wasn't being more forthcoming. The thought made her heart ache, and her defenses tightened reflexively. What right did he have to think she should confide in him? He'd never been exactly an open emotional book himself.

But she couldn't resist trying to erase that disappointed look on his face. "Besides, I love producing. I want to do something that makes a difference. Anyone can just read the news. I like being able to have a say in which stories make air and how they're written. I like knowing I solved a dozen last-minute problems and helped put a newscast on the air. And most importantly, I like the feeling I get when we run a story that really makes a difference in people's lives."

Stone nodded sympathetically. "I can understand that. But you're still making a difference in people's lives, Jamie. The way you read the news makes them care about the stories." He ran a hand across his chin. "Besides, whether you know it or not, you're making a big difference in the lives of your co-workers. You're attracting viewers in droves, and the station desperately needs that. It's up for sale, and if the ratings don't improve, whoever buys this place will clean house and bring on their own staff."

She stood stock-still and stared at him. "I had no idea that anyone's job depended on me. Why didn't you tell me before now?"

He lifted his shoulders. "I didn't want to put any additional pressure on you. Besides, if things go as planned, that scenario will never materialize."

"I never wanted to put anyone's job in jeopardy." She reached out and hesitantly placed her hand on his arm. "Including yours. I mean, I didn't wear the sweat suit or drag you out on the dance floor because I wanted to sabotage your career."

He caught her gaze and held it, his pupils darkening until his eyes looked almost black. "I'm glad to hear that, Jamie." His voice was low and husky, and tension coiled between them like a taut spring.

He slowly reached out and lifted a strand of her hair, sifting it through his fingers. It was an old, familiar gesture and it made her breath catch in her throat.

She searched her mind for something to say that would neutralize the emotion sizzling between them. "Speaking of affecting lives—did you get my memo about the children's series?"

"Yes. I like your ideas for the format." He pulled back his hand and jammed it in his pocket. "What's the next step?"

"I'm meeting with the social worker at the orphanage Monday afternoon."

"I'll go with you. We can talk about the series on the way." He glanced at the studio clock, then gazed at her. "I've got a meeting with the assignment editor in two minutes. But if you want to wait for me, I'll take you to lunch when I finish."

The invitation caught her off guard—but then, so had everything else that had happened between them. He smiled at her, his dark eyes glittering, his face wearing that intent expression he used to reserve just for her. She knew it was an invitation to more than just lunch.

He wanted to pick up where they'd left off last night. His gaze captured hers and electricity buzzed between them, making her light-headed and heavy-footed. She was sorely tempted to say yes. When he looked at her like that, it was hard to remember that only heartache would result from getting involved with him again.

But it would, she reminded herself. The differences that had torn them apart were still there, glaring and large and unresolved, and no amount of physical attraction would overcome them.

"I'm having lunch with Grams," she finally managed.

He gave a slow, soft smile that exposed his roguish dimple. She might be off the hook this time, but the look in his eyes told her the issue was far from settled. "Okay, Jamie. But don't forget you agreed to have dinner with me on Monday. And you'd better not dream up any excuses to get out of it, because I won't take no for an answer."

He smiled again and sauntered out of the studio. Even after the door banged shut behind him, she could still feel his presence. His words lingered in her mind, his scent filled her nostrils, his touch imprinted her skin, making her senses reel and her heart long for more.

Damn him! He'd always had that effect on her. It wasn't fair that he could still make her feel this way when he'd broken her heart so thoroughly.

The conclusion she'd reached this morning was certainly true as far as the attraction between them was concerned, she thought ruefully.

Nothing had changed. Nothing at all.

"You certainly seem distracted today, dear," Grams remarked as the waiter handed them menus and flitted away. "Does it have anything to do with your evening with Stone?"

Jamie looked at her grandmother and nervously took a sip of water. Grams's overly nonchalant manner was a dead giveaway that the elderly woman was positively vibrating with curiosity. So this was the reason her grandmother had called and invited her to lunch.

Jamie opted to play dumb. "What do you mean?"

Grams unfolded the large linen napkin and primly placed it in her lap. "Well, I took Lulu for a walk last night and

I couldn't help but notice his car parked in your driveway. It was late. And the only light on in the house seemed to be coming from your bedroom.''

Jamie nearly choked on her drink. She set down the glass, coughed, then picked it up and drained it, hoping the icy liquid would counterbalance the heat rushing to her face.

Grams's eyes were bright, and Jamie knew there was no way her grandmother was going to let her dodge the issue. She set down the glass and eyed her sternly.

"Cut the innocent act, Grams. You're about as convincing as those professional wrestlers you watch on television. You and Lulu were prowling the streets in the middle of the night?''

Grams gave an exaggerated shrug. "I can't control little Lulu's kidney functions. When she has to go, she has to go.''

"What happened to her litter box?''

"She's very fastidious. She prefers the great outdoors.''

"Uh-huh. And I suppose she had a fastidious urge to go right in front of my house.''

"It's one of her favorite spots.''

"Admit it, Grams. You were spying on me.''

Grams picked up the menu and opened it with a flourish. "If you don't want to talk about it, fine.''

"Fine.''

Grams managed to wait five full seconds before she lowered the menu and eagerly leaned forward over it. "But if you're getting back together with Stone, I want you to know I wholeheartedly approve.''

Jamie pushed a strand of hair behind her ear and sighed. "We're not getting back together.''

Grams's smile faded, along with the twinkle in her eye. She was clearly crestfallen. "Why on earth not, dear? They say love is always better the second time around.''

Jamie rolled her eyes. "This is real life, not a soap opera, Grams. And the major problem that broke us up hasn't changed. If anything, Stone's new career as a consultant demands even more of his time, not to mention a more transient life-style. I don't want to live that way."

Grams's gaze was sharp enough to nail Jamie to her chair. "You want to go on as you have been, living without him?"

Pain, hot and sudden, shot through Jamie's chest. It lodged somewhere near her heart and burned like a blazing arrow, illuminating the empty space that had ached inside ever since she and Stone had separated.

It wasn't a question Jamie wanted to ask herself, much less discuss. It raised possibilities that just weren't possible, made it seem as if she had options other than the lonely one she'd lived with for the past three years. To allow herself to seriously consider reuniting with Stone was to open herself to another round of heartache, and she just didn't know if she could stand it.

Jamie shifted her weight on the chair and gazed out at the crowded restaurant. "I really don't want to talk about this, Grams. Can we please change the topic?"

Grams gave her an injured, long-suffering look. "My only concern is your happiness, Jamie. But if you want to talk about something else, fine." Grams took a dainty sip of water. "So how are things between you and Stone at work?"

Despite her roiling emotions, Jamie couldn't help but laugh at the old woman's incorrigibility. Grams might not have changed the subject, but at least she'd moved it out of the bedroom.

Which was exactly what she needed to do with her relationship with Stone, Jamie thought decisively.

Still, the question Grams had posed resounded in Jamie's mind for the rest of the day, and she found herself unwittingly pondering it off and on throughout the weekend.

Chapter Seven

Jamie checked her watch as she hurried down the station hallway Monday afternoon. She had a stack of correspondence waiting on her desk and she was due to leave for the children's home in less than an hour.

With Stone. Just the thought of him made her pulse accelerate. Not only was he going to accompany her to the meeting with the social worker, he was also taking her to dinner tonight.

Why, oh why, had she agreed to a dinner date with the man? Spending time with him was playing havoc with her mental and emotional health. Every time she saw him, her nerves grew more jangled, her emotions more confused.

Even when she didn't see him, he managed to disrupt her life. Thoughts of him had plagued her all weekend despite her best efforts to focus on the gardening seminar. If she didn't keep her distance, she'd never survive Stone's stint at the station.

More to the point, she'd never survive his departure from it.

She couldn't allow herself to think about it, she resolved. She'd keep her attention focused squarely on the series and off anything personal. She couldn't afford to do anything that might escalate the attraction between Stone and her. From now on, whenever she saw Stone, she'd comport herself as a paragon of professionalism.

Immersed in her thoughts, she rounded the corner and bumped squarely into Todd. She swallowed back the distaste that filled her throat and forced a smile. ''Good morning, Todd.''

He responded with a silent glare.

His animosity hit her like a blast of icy air, sending a chill chasing through her. She'd managed to avoid him since the night of the Arts Ball, but avoidance wasn't the solution. They were bound to encounter each other as long as they both worked at the same station. She needed to do something to defuse his hostility, and she needed to do it fast.

She had an idea she was sure would work. She'd intended to run it by Stone before she mentioned it, but the venom in Todd's stare made her decide to talk to him about it now. She laid a hand on his arm. ''Todd, I know you've been given a raw deal, and I want to help make it up to you. I'm working on a project right now that could put you back in the spotlight.''

He raised a skeptical eyebrow. ''Oh, yeah?''

''Yes.'' Jamie nodded encouragingly. ''We're starting a new weekly series featuring children who are up for adoption, and we need a reporter to handle it—someone with a lot of charisma, someone who's a recognized personality. It's going to be highly promoted, and I think it would be a good way for you to get back in the limelight. Are you interested?''

''Well, sure.'' His rheumy eyes were suspicious. ''But what makes you think they'll let me do it?''

''I'm producing the series, so I should have some say on the talent. I'll make a case for you if you're interested.''

''Yeah, I'm interested.''

Jamie smiled. ''Good. Stone and I are finalizing the details now. I should have an answer for you by the first of next week." She patted his arm. "I'll do my best for you, Todd." She turned and hurried down the hall, sparing him the necessity of thanking her or apologizing, knowing neither came easily to Todd.

The offer had seemed to placate him, she thought with satisfaction as she settled at her desk. She was confident Stone would go along with it. After all, the series had been written into her contract only at her insistence. Since Stone had said it wouldn't have any impact on ratings, surely he'd let her decide who the reporter would be.

"Ready?"

An hour later, Jamie glanced up from the stack of correspondence to see Stone leaning over her desk. Her breath caught at the sight of him and she looked away, reminding herself of her resolve to keep their relationship purely business oriented. But her heart pounded in a very unbusinesslike manner as she gathered up her purse and a leather notebook and walked with him across the newsroom.

Stone held the door for her. "You're the talk of the town, Jamie. Mr. Milton is beside himself with joy at your newfound popularity."

Jamie grimaced as they stepped into the parking lot. She'd spent most of Friday and the better part of her morning dealing with the fallout from her new celebrity status—letters, cards and phone calls requesting everything from political support to a lock of her hair. Even at the gardening seminar she'd had to fend off requests for autographs and photos. All the unwelcome attention unnerved her, and she couldn't wait for her two months at the anchor desk to be over.

"The topic is kind of a sore subject with me," she said. "Can we talk about the children's series instead?"

"Sure." Stone opened her door, then circled the vehicle and climbed in himself. "Do you have a name for it?"

"I thought we might call it 'A Home of My Own.'"

Stone nodded thoughtfully as he guided the vehicle onto the street. "Sounds good. It has a lot of emotional appeal."

A rush of pleasure pulsed through Jamie's veins. Part of her had been afraid he was going to pay only lip service to her ideas. She flipped open her notebook, feeling her shoulders relax. "As I mentioned in the memo, I see us showcasing a different child every week."

"What sort of visuals do you have in mind?"

"It depends on the interests of the individual child. I have a whole list of possible situations and locations—playing in a park, going horseback riding, throwing a Frisbee, going to an amusement park, flying a kite..."

"Will this primarily be a VO?" Stone asked.

Jamie nodded. "We'll use a voice-over as we run some of the footage, but we'll probably use some nat sound, too. The key part of each story—the part I see as being the series's signature—will be a sound bite of the child talking about his or her hopes and dreams."

Stone took his eyes from the road long enough to meet hers and grin. "I like it. Sounds like you've thought it all out." He turned onto a side street. "You'll be great at this, Jamie."

"Thanks." Delight at the unexpected compliment poured over her like a ray of sunshine. She shouldn't care so much about Stone's opinion, she warned herself sternly. The amount of pleasure she felt as a result of his casual remark was entirely inappropriate for a business relationship.

She was also deriving entirely too much pleasure from looking at his face. She glanced away, only to have her gaze land on his hands on the steering wheel. Her heart turned over as she took in the faint dusting of hair across his knuckles, the tan skin, the clean clipped nails.

And the finger where he used to wear his wedding ring.

A lump unexpectedly formed in her throat. When they were married, he'd never taken it off. Early in their marriage she'd offered to polish it for him and he'd refused to remove it. "It's a permanent part of me now," he'd replied. "Just like you."

Jamie swallowed, her mouth dry. At what point had that changed? When they separated? When she filed for divorce? Or had he taken his ring off when she'd removed hers—when he got the final decree?

She thought of her own wedding band, ensconced in a box at the bottom of her jewelry case, untouched since the day she'd tearfully taken it off.

Did he even still have his ring? If not, what had he done with it?

She was mortified to realize that tears threatened her eyes. She stared out the window, not daring to blink for fear they'd spill down her cheeks, and tried to regain control of her emotions.

She'd been confused and unsettled about their relationship ever since the night of the Arts Ball, the ''what ifs'' spinning around in her mind like hamsters in a caged wheel. Grams's pointed question had only served to heighten the sense of chaos.

If they both hadn't been so stubborn, if she hadn't issued that ultimatum, could she and Stone have saved their marriage?

It was useless to think along those lines, she reprimanded herself. Stone's work was his first love, and unless she were willing to play second fiddle to his career, there could be no future for them. That was an immutable fact, the problem their divorce document referred to as ''irreconcilable difference.'' She'd be a fool to forget it for even a moment.

She shouldn't have agreed to have dinner with him tonight. There was no point in getting things started again when there was no way of resolving the issue.

''Stone, about tonight...''

He glanced at her. ''I'm looking forward to it. Where would you like to go?''

''I've been thinking. I don't think it's a good idea for us to see each other outside of work.''

''We've covered this ground, Jamie. I hate to eat alone, and from the looks of your freezer, you could use a good meal, too. What about Mexican?''

His smile was contagious. Jamie found herself grinning back at him. The prospect of an evening in his company was irresistible. "You're not playing fair. You know how I love Mexican food."

"Whatever made you think I'd play fair? You know the old saying about love and war."

"Which is this, Stone?"

He gave a cryptic smile. "Don't you know?"

Her heart skipped like a flat rock on a pond. Was he trying to sound her out, or was he simply teasing? She decided to play it safe. "*I* was asking *you*."

Stone steered the car through the redbrick gate of the children's home. "Why, it's both, Jamie." His tone was light, but the expression in his eyes was not. "It's both."

"Who likes to play games?" Jamie asked.

"I do! I do!" The eight children seated around her on the playground lawn each raised a hand, bouncing up and down in excitement.

Stone leaned against the tall brick fence surrounding the grounds and smiled. The children had started out shy and quiet, but Jamie had managed to draw them out of their shells in record time.

He'd had an opportunity to watch her in action as a producer during the past two hours, something he'd never actually seen before. They'd worked at the same stations in the past, but never in the same department. She'd always been in children's programming, and he'd always been in news.

She was good—damned good. As he'd watched her iron out the details of the series during a tour of the facility and a meeting with Mrs. Mathis, the social worker assigned to the project, he'd grown more and more impressed. Jamie seemed to have thought of everything, including several issues that never would have occurred to him—how to keep the children from feeling disappointed if the story failed to result in their placement in a home, how to keep the children who weren't featured from feeling overlooked or second-best, and how to explain their special needs on the air without embarrassing them.

Her concern for the children moved him, and his chest tightened as he watched her. He should probably feel guilty. Her attention was focused on the needs of others, while he was caught up in a purely selfish concern: could he ever make her care for him again?

"She has a way with children, doesn't she?" Mrs. Mathis asked.

"Yes," Stone replied, looking at the rapt faces of the boys and girls sitting around her.

"Peter, what do you like to play?" Jamie asked.

"Power Rangers!" The blond-headed tyke in a leg brace jumped up and illustrated several martial arts moves.

Stone grinned, but his chest felt like a steel band was constricting around it. He used to imagine Jamie as the mother of his children, used to picture her belly round with child, used to fantasize about what their offspring might look like. She would make a wonderful mother. She had the attentiveness and warmth that had been lacking from his own youth, that his own overworked, harried mother had been too exhausted to provide, that he wanted for his own children. Providing solid financial security for her and the family they'd someday have together had been the reason he worked so hard during their marriage.

He'd tried time and time again to tell her that, but she'd dismissed all of his comments as platitudes.

She thought he was like her own father, full of empty promises and endless somedays. He'd never been able to convince her that his drive to succeed wasn't just a selfish ego trip, that he intended to stop and settle down once he got his career launched. She'd insisted that actions spoke louder than words, that none of his actions indicated he'd ever be happy unless he were constantly striving for greater and greater financial success.

His fingers crumpled into fists by his side. He'd intended his career to be a means to an end, not the end in itself. How had he managed to mess things up so royally? Jamie had certainly been right about one thing; success had made a lonely bedfellow these past three years. He'd buried him-

self in his work and avoided examining his feelings about
it, but seeing Jamie again had made all the emptiness, all
the loneliness, all the pain float to the surface.

Maybe she'd give him a second chance. When he'd seen
the music box in her bedroom, a tenderness he'd thought
dead and gone had revived in his chest, and hope had
soared from the ashes of his heart like the legendary phoenix. Until that moment, he hadn't known what he wanted,
hadn't been sure what he felt, but as those tiny figures
twirled and that tinny music spilled into the air, he'd looked
into her eyes and seen everything he'd ever wanted in life.

He knew she still had feelings for him, too. She'd responded too deeply to his kisses, too passionately to his
touch not to care.

He couldn't leave it alone. He couldn't leave *her* alone.
He wanted her back in his life.

A bell rang, and the other children on the playground
formed a line into the building. Stone watched Jamie stand
and wave as the circle around her dispersed, then bend to
talk to a small boy with dark curls who lingered behind.
She crouched beside him, her hand on his shoulder, the
expression on her face so gentle and understanding it made
his heart ache. She gave the child a hug and watched him
scamper off to join his classmates, then turned and headed
to where he and the social worker were standing.

"What a great group of children!" Jamie turned to Mrs.
Mathis. "I'd love to feature all of them."

The older woman smiled. "The only one I have reser-
vations about is the little boy you were just talking with.
Michael is an adorable child, but I'm afraid he might not
come across well on television, especially since you want
the children to talk. He has a speech impediment. When he
gets excited or nervous, he can't get a word out."

"I noticed." Jamie's fingers nervously toyed with her
purse strap. "It's nothing we can't work around. We could
shoot the whole segment as a voice-over."

"Voice-over?"

"We'd show footage of him while the reporter talks about him. He wouldn't have to speak."

Mrs. Martin nodded. "He's very shy. But if he's agreeable, it's fine with me."

Jamie smiled. "Good. I'd hate to see his problem keep him from having the same opportunities as the other children." She hesitated, her expression growing solemn. "Is he getting help? I know a little bit about speech impediments, and therapy c-can make a b-b-big d-d-di-dif—" Jamie halted and drew a deep breath "—improvement."

Stone glanced at her in surprise, noting her reddened face. It was the first time he'd ever heard even a hint of stuttering from her. But then, he'd never actually heard her discuss the topic before; she'd always managed to change the subject. He regarded her thoughtfully, recalling that Grams had told him talking about stuttering was the one thing that made it recur. A protective urge welled up within him, and he took her arm, giving it a squeeze.

"One of the counselors here is trying to work with him, but she's not a licensed therapist," Mrs. Mathis replied. "I'm afraid our budget is very limited."

"That's something my consulting firm may be able to help with," Stone interjected. "Why don't you get some cost figures together and let me know what you need?"

Mrs. Mathis's face creased in a smile. "I'll be more than happy to do that. Thank you, Mr. Johnson."

"It was kind of you to offer to help with Michael's speech therapy," Jamie said later as they drove back to the station.

Stone glanced at her. "No problem." He turned his eyes back to the road, looking for a way to broach a topic he knew was difficult for her.

"In all the time I've known you, Jamie, I've never heard you stutter before." He glanced at her again. Her spine was rigid and her face was averted, but a pink stain spread across her neck above her beige jacket.

Her silence grew loud as he waited for her reply. "I wish

you'd tell me about your speech impediment and how you got over it. If your friend hadn't happened to mention it, I never would have known you'd had a problem."

"I'll take that as a compliment."

Her tone held a forced lightness. She was trying to divert him from the subject, but he wasn't going to let her.

This was something he needed her to talk about, something he should have insisted on three years ago. He wasn't very good at this intimacy stuff, but all his instincts told him that if he wanted a chance at rebuilding their relationship, he had to make her trust him. If he could make her give up her secrets, maybe her heart would follow. "I wish you'd tell me about it, Jamie. I want to know you, to understand you. Part of you has always kept me at arm's length. You never really let me get close, not even when we were married."

"I wouldn't let you close?" She turned toward him, her face flushed, her eyes wide and incredulous. "How could you get close when you were never around?"

He wouldn't allow himself to be drawn into the old argument. "What kind of therapy should Michael be getting?"

Jamie gazed out the window. "I don't know if I can talk about this."

"Why not, Jamie?"

"I d-d-don't want to stutter in front of you," she mumbled.

It was the answer Stone expected, and it ravaged his heart. It spoke of mistrust. It placed him in the category of polite stranger. He remembered what it felt like to run his hands over her bare skin, knew how she called out in the throes of passion, recalled exactly what temperature she liked her bathwater. Why had she shut him out of her life in this area, when they'd been intimate in so many others?

Something deep inside told him he needed to break through her armor on this issue. If he were ever to have a chance of winning her back, he had to gain her trust. Somehow he had to wedge his way into her mind and heart. "What would be so terrible about that?"

She looked down at her hands. "I d-don't want you to see me like this."

"Like what, Jamie?"

She drew a deep, rattly breath. The silence stretched out, broken only by the whoosh of the wind rushing by the car and the bump of the tires over the expansion joints in the highway pavement. He'd given up hope of an answer when her answer came.

"De-de-defective."

"Defective? Is that what you thought I'd think?" He braked hard and made a tight turn, steering the Jeep onto a side street. He pulled into an office building parking lot and killed the engine.

"Jamie..." He grasped her upper arms and stared into her eyes. "Where ever did you get an idea like that?"

She shrugged and gazed down at her hands in her lap, where her fingers were twisting and untwisting.

"Jamie, do you really think I'm that shallow? My God, honey—do you have any idea how I felt about you? How I still feel about you?"

When she lifted her eyes, they were large and moist and filled with something he couldn't quite name. Fear, longing, sadness, hope? All of the above, but mostly fear.

Was he scaring her off, coming on too strong? Or was she just afraid of stuttering in front of him? Either way, it killed him to think he'd put that look in those incredible blue eyes.

"Talk to me, Jamie," he pleaded.

She gulped and looked away.

He touched her chin gently and turned her face toward his, forcing her to meet his gaze. "Jamie, I don't give a damn if you stutter. I won't think any less of you for it. But I'll sure be disappointed if you don't have the guts to level with me. I always thought you had a lot of courage." He pulled back and gave a shrug. "But maybe I was wrong.'' If there was one thing she'd never been able to stand, it was being called a coward. He counted on it now.

Heat flashed in her eyes, and her spine stiffened. She drew away and stared out the windshield. "My father c-called my stuttering a de-de-defect. He m-made me feel like d-d-damaged g-goods. He t-t-told me t-t-to just k-keep my mouth shut if I c-c-couldn't t-t-talk without st-st-stuttering. He used to send me t-t-to my room if I st-st-stuttered.'' She drew a deep, shaky breath. "He said I had to g-g-get over it or no one w-w-would ever w-want to hire me or b-be friends with me or l-l-l-l-l-love me.'' She hung her head, causing her hair to fall over her cheeks.

"Why, that no-good son of a—'' Stone caught himself before he completed the muttered oath. This was Jamie's father they were talking about, he reminded himself. The sorry S.O.B. didn't deserve a child like Jamie, but it wouldn't help matters to say so in front of her. Stone only wished the bastard were still alive so he could punch him in the mouth.

Stone reached out and pulled her to him, getting as close as he could with the gearbox between them. "Jamie, honey, you don't believe that, do you?''

"Not anymore. N-not intellectually. But emotionally....'' She gave a small shrug. "I hate to st-st-stutter. It m-m-makes me feel s-so—'' she hesitated and drew a long, shaky breath "—out of control. And a-a-ashamed.''

If anyone should be ashamed, it was her father. Stone tamped down his anger, knowing it wasn't what Jamie needed now. She needed acceptance, understanding, love.

She needed him.

"Jamie, honey, it doesn't make you defective. It makes you human.'' He rubbed his palms up and down her arms. "Everyone has problems. Some people's problems just aren't as readily apparent as others.''

He was rewarded with a wry, tremulous smile. He'd better press ahead while she was willing to talk.

"Tell me how you got over it,'' he urged. She hesitated,

and he deliberately tugged at her heartstrings. "I'd like to have some idea of what Michael needs to do."

She breathed deeply. "I w-worked with a therapist who specialized in relaxation t-t-techniques. My t-t-type of stuttering is caused by t-t-tension in the vocal cords." She gave a sheepish laugh. "As you can t-t-tell, it's usually hard c-c-consonants that make me stumble. And once the stuttering gets started, it's hard to st-stop."

"What do you do when that happens?"

"F-f-first I t-try to substitute a word that's easier t-t-to say than the one I'm st-st-stuck on. Some st-st-stutterers get so g-good at word substitution that most people d-d-don't even know they have a problem. B-b-but one thing that's always d-d-dif-difi—*hard*—is saying my name. There's no way to substitute another word for that."

Stone stared at her, a sense of amazement and admiration flowing through him. He'd had no idea of the scope of her problem. Hell, until his conversation with Grams the other evening, he hadn't had a clue it still bothered her. He'd thought she'd gotten over it completely, like a case of childhood chicken pox.

Or maybe he'd never really internalized the fact she'd had a problem in the first place. The thought filled him with chagrin. He didn't like the idea of how little she'd trusted him or how insensitive he'd been to her.

He wanted to make up for lost time. Learning all he could about her problem now seemed like a good place to start. "What type of relaxation techniques did you learn?"

"Controlling airflow, slowing d-down my speech pattern, relaxing my body, deep breathing—but mainly how to concentrate. Thinking and worrying about stuttering make it a self-fulfilling prophecy. I learned to focus my attention on the subject under d-discussion instead of on my delivery. But when the subject under discussion is stuttering, well…" she gave a rueful smile "…that presents a d-d-dilemma."

"How long did it take you to get over it?"

"As you c-c-can see, I'm not—not entirely. It improved a lot after a year of therapy, but it's a lifelong process."

All of Jamie's attempts to get off the air, her extraordinary concentration at the anchor desk, suddenly fell into place. Stone ran a finger lightly down her cheek. "Is this why you don't want to be on camera?" he asked softly.

Her eyes met his, then slid away. "Y-yes."

Stone dropped his hand and muttered an oath. "Damn it, Jamie, I wish you'd told me. Now you're locked into that contract and there's no way Milton is going to let you out of it."

She regarded him warily. "If I'd told you earlier, would it have made a difference?"

"Of course it would have, damn it!"

"You would have kept me off the air?"

"I would have done my darnedest." His voice was adamant, his eyes intent and sincere.

She looked away, her heart tripping wildly. Would he have really? And if so, would it have been because he cared for her personally, or because he was looking out for the station's interests?

He stretched his arm behind her on the back of the seat and gently fingered her shoulder. "Jamie, honey, it's too late to change things now. But you haven't had a hint of trouble on the air. You're doing a terrific job."

"Except for that brief lapse in fashion sense," she said dryly.

Stone laughed and rubbed her arm. "You impress the hell out of me, Jamie," he said softly. "Do you know that?"

The admiration in his eyes poured over her, melting her resistance to him like hot fudge on an ice-cream sundae. Relief pumped through her veins, along with something like a runner's high—a light-headedness, a giddiness, an exultant sense of freedom at having finally shared her secret. It reminded her of the way she used to feel in childhood on the first day it was finally warm enough to play outside without wearing a winter coat.

His fingers toyed with the fabric of her jacket. "I don't know if you even noticed it, but as you got caught up in telling me about your stuttering, you stopped doing it."

Her grin felt like it reached both ears. "I did, didn't I?"

"You darn sure did." He tightened his arm around her and leaned closer. Attraction sparked, then blazed between them. They sat, simply looking at each other, as the air in the Jeep grew warmer. Desire curled around them like smoke from a campfire, and Jamie's lips quivered as her gaze fell to his mouth.

The space between them was slowly closing, and she knew she was about to be kissed.

She should protest, her mind told her. She should just say no. If she had any logic at all, she'd turn away.

But logic had fled. A sense of intimacy wrapped her up with him like a blanket. She felt known as she'd never been known before. She felt connected and close to him, and her heart longed to get closer still.

Jamie watched Stone draw nearer, his eyes asking permission. Hers granted it as her lids fluttered closed. His mouth grazed hers, his lips warm and firm and tender. The kiss was achingly sweet, as gentle as a butterfly on a flower, and her heart blossomed under it, opening for him. Her lips did the same.

He twined his fingers in her hair and slanted his mouth across hers, deepening the kiss. She reached her arms around his back, losing herself in the hard feel of his body, the seductive slide of his lips on hers, the warm knowledge she'd just shared a part of herself with him that she'd never entrusted to anyone.

She was sinking deep into a fog of exquisite sensation when a vehicle sputtered to a noisy stop in the parking slot beside them. A moment later a car door slammed shut, the sound as loud and jarring as a gunshot, making Jamie jump and jerk open her eyes.

A middle-aged woman with brassy blond hair and cat-eyed glasses stared through the side window, clutching her purse to her chest. "Look, Harry. Isn't that the lady on the news?"

The woman leaned forward and rapped on the glass. "Yoo hoo!" she sing-songed in a high, nasal voice. A man with a bulbous nose joined her at the window.

"Oh, no," Jamie moaned, hiding her face in her hands.

Stone slid into position behind the steering wheel and started the engine. "Excuse us, we're trying to pull out," he bellowed, motioning with his arm.

"Harry, it *is* the newslady!" the woman screeched. "And that man had his lips all over her—in broad daylight, no less!"

Stone backed out of the parking place, laying rubber.

"How embarrassing," Jamie murmured as they pulled into the street.

Stone cut her a rakish grin. "Don't worry about it. The only thing that old biddy has had on her lips in the last quarter century is prune juice."

Jamie laughed, and Stone's deep rumble joined her. The sound of their mingled laughter danced in the air, conjuring poignant memories.

He glanced at her, his eyes as dark and tempting as Godiva chocolates. "It reminds me of the time we were caught in the break room in Tulsa. Do you remember?"

How could she forget? Just the thought of it made her cheeks burn. They'd been kissing like they had today, her back braced against the soda machine, her legs wrapped around Stone's thighs.

"It was a good thing that photographer came in when he did instead of five minutes later. God, I wanted you, Jamie." He reached across the console and took her hand. "I still do."

Her pulse rate skittered into the ozone layer. "We were always physically compatible."

"Compatible? More like combustible." He took his eyes from the road and looked at her, his gaze hot and frank and hungry. A shiver of heat raced through her and settled low in her belly. "It's never been that way with anyone else, Jamie."

"Do you have a lot of basis for comparison?" Mercy, that sounded catty, but she couldn't help it. She had to know.

"Not since you."

Nothing he could have said would have pleased her more. There had been no one else in her life, either.

Suppressing a delighted grin, she gazed out the window and thought of the few times she'd dated in the past three years. Each time, she'd found herself comparing the man to Stone. Each time, she'd spent the evening watching the clock, waiting for the earliest possible moment to plead fatigue and ask to be taken home. Each time, she'd wondered why on earth she'd agreed to go out with the man in the first place.

Once, as an experiment, she'd let a date kiss her goodnight. Instead of the knee-weakening desire Stone's kisses had always stirred, she'd only felt an overpowering urge to wipe her mouth and gargle.

She glanced over at Stone's profile. He caught her eye and smiled, and the contact made her heart skip a beat.

No one but Stone had ever had this effect on her. He made her feel vibrant and alive, as if her life had suddenly switched from black-and-white to vivid color.

She gazed out at the passing scenery, her emotions ricocheting between scared to death and strangely at ease, and wondered nervously what the night ahead would bring.

Chapter Eight

"Umm, this is delicious," Jamie murmured, swallowing the last bite of sopaipilla and licking the honey off her fingers.

Stone leaned back in his chair and grinned. "I've missed watching you do that. But then, I've missed watching you do a lot of things."

Jamie averted her eyes, not wanting him to know the impact his words had on her heart rate, and stared out at the crowded restaurant. It had been a wonderful evening, an evening full of jokes and laughter and engrossing conversation. Jamie couldn't remember the last time she'd enjoyed anyone's company as much. They'd talked about current events, they'd caught up on each other lives, they'd flirted and reminisced and reestablished the easy, teasing rapport that had always made their relationship sparkle.

The tone of the evening had been lighthearted, but a current of serious attraction sizzled just beneath the surface.

It had been sizzling ever since their encounter in the parking lot. If Stone had not had to go back to the station for the five- and six-o'clock newscasts, heaven only knew what might have happened then.

Stone gave her a slow, sexy half smile across the table. There was no mistaking the thoughts behind his expression, and the possibilities made her blood race.

His eyes rested on her face, his gaze as warm as his hand covering hers on the table. "You were wonderful with those children today, Jamie." He flashed his irresistible dimple, and she felt the warmth spread south. "You're going to be great on the air with them."

"On the air?" Incredulous, Jamie stared at him. "What are you talking about?"

Stone's eyes narrowed. "What do you mean, what am I talking about?"

The sopaipilla suddenly turned to lead in her stomach. "I'm the producer of the series, not the talent."

Stone's fingers tightened over her hers. "You're both, Jamie."

A cold sense of dread seized her. "If this is a joke, it's not funny, Stone. My contract says the series will run for at least six months, whether I'm still an anchor or not."

Stone nodded. "That's right. And it also says you're the reporter on the series for as long as it airs."

Her body froze as her mind raced. Oh, mercy—did it? How could she have overlooked it? She should have taken that blasted contract to an attorney.

She yanked her hand out from under his. "Why the heck didn't you tell me?"

"Jamie, honey, I thought you knew."

His expression was open, his tone sincere. Dadblast it! She'd been so flustered during the contract negotiations that the clause had evidently escaped her notice.

Maybe she could change his mind now. "I want to be off the air altogether when my anchor contract is up. Why don't we let Todd handle the series?"

"Todd?" It was Stone's turn to sound incredulous. "Jamie, there's no way. Can you honestly see Todd interacting with those children?"

Jamie bit her bottom lip. "I could make it work. I'd script everything out for him."

"You'd have to do more than that. You'd have to choreograph his every move, send him to charm school and put a bag over his head."

Jamie was not amused. Her chin tilted stubbornly. "I'm used to working with him. I could make it work."

Stone shook his head. "It's out of the question, Jamie. Your on-air charisma was the selling point for the series, and if you refuse to do it, Mr. Milton will cancel the concept altogether." Stone's forehead creased in concern as he regarded her. "If you're worried about not having enough time to handle the on-air responsibilities and produce the series, too, we can assign another producer."

"Assign another producer? Over my dead body!" She bristled like a cornered porcupine. "If you think I'd hand the series over to some hack producer who's only interested in throwing something on the air and doesn't care about finding homes for these children, then you need to think again. We've got to convince people to become adoptive parents, and that means these stories have to be special. They need to be emotionally moving, they need to be accurate, they need to be sensitive..."

"I know you'll do a great job, Jamie."

"Besides," she continued hotly, "I intend to work as a producer long after this anchor nonsense has run its course. I need to keep my hand in. I'm not about to give up the only concession I got in that entire blasted contract."

Stone held up his hands in a gesture of surrender. "I'm not trying to talk you out of it. I was just worried about your workload."

"Is there anything else in my contract I need to know about?"

"Do you have a copy of it at your house?" he asked.

"Yes."

"Good." Stone raised his hand and signaled the waiter for the check. "We'll review it together."

The contract was the last thing Stone wanted to think about as he sat beside Jamie on her sofa an hour later. They were seated close together, close enough to both read the same page at the same time, close enough that the scent of her shampoo teased his nostrils and the heat of her body beckoned him even closer. Her arm brushed his chest as she flipped to the last page, and his thoughts flew off on an erotic tangent.

But Jamie's attention was riveted on the contract, her brow furrowed into a frown and her lips pressed into a tight line. Stone heaved a sigh. They'd gone over every *therefore,* every *herewith,* and every *aforementioned.* They'd gone over the doggone thing word by word and clause by clause, and Jamie had grown increasingly tense with every line. The evening was not taking the turn Stone had intended.

Thrusting the document aside, Jamie stood and paced in front of her tiny fireplace. "According to the contract, you've got me, fair and square." Her voice was tight and angry. "What I want or don't want doesn't matter in the least."

"I didn't know you were worried about stuttering when we drafted this, Jamie." Stone fought to keep the frustration out of his voice. "If you recall, I thought I was helping you by getting the children's series included in it at all. Mr. Milton didn't care for the concept. And if you refuse to be the reporter, he's sure to cancel it altogether."

"But we can't let him do that! We can't let those children down." She placed her hands on her hips and glared at him. "Whether you understood my stuttering problem or not, you should have had more consideration for my feelings. Why the heck did you have to force me on the air in the first place?"

Stone ran a hand down his face. "Jamie, we've covered this ground before."

"You're darn right we've covered this ground before. Given the choice between your ambition and my feelings, ambition wins every time. Even when I was your wife, you were really married to the almighty dollar."

"It wasn't that way at all, Jamie."

"No? Then what way was it?"

He stood and shoved his hands in his pockets, wondering what to do. Lord, he hated it when she got angry like this. The same cold, scared, shut-out feeling he used to get as a child would grip his gut.

Maybe he should just leave. It was the way he used to handle conflict with her.

And look where it had gotten him, he thought ruefully.

He sighed heavily. No, if he wanted to win her back, he'd have to come up with another approach. He gazed at her, hoping to find a clue.

She was standing ramrod straight, her rigid posture a barricade to approachability. Maybe her anger was just a barricade, too. Maybe the real issue wasn't anger, but fear.

Fear of letting him close. Fear of letting him back in her life.

They'd made strides in that direction today when she'd opened up to him about her stuttering. Their relationship had somehow shifted to higher, more solid ground. The evening had been wonderful, almost magical until she discovered she was the on-air talent for the series. And then here they were, right back where they'd started, muddling around again in the same old quagmire.

He rubbed his jaw. If he was ever going to get through to her, maybe he'd have to open up, too.

The thought made his stomach clench. How the hell was he supposed to open up to her when she was angry? His instinctive response to anyone's wrath was to withdraw and detach. It was a reaction that ran bone deep, a survival technique he'd learned in childhood, a defense against his father's temper.

But detachment hadn't worked well in marriage, and it sure as heck wouldn't fix things now.

He looked at Jamie as she stood stiffly by the mantel, her fine golden hair streaming down her back, her delicate profile contrasted against the brick of the fireplace, her back as straight as the brass poker in the stand by her feet. Lord, she was lovely. If he wanted her back, change had to start somewhere.

Might as well be right here, right now, Stone thought. If he wanted to reestablish a relationship with her, he'd have to change the way he responded to her.

It was time to fish or cut bait. He stepped up beside her, drew a deep breath and waded in. "I'm not like your father, Jamie. I'm not on a power trip, I don't care about status symbols and I don't need to be rich. I just want to make sure I'm never poor again like I was as a boy."

He braced both hands against the mantel, weighing how much to tell her. His upbringing had been so different from hers that he was afraid the full truth would repel her.

She knew his parents hadn't been wealthy, that he'd grown up in a small town in southeastern Oklahoma, that he'd worked his way through college by holding down two jobs during the school year and working summers as a ranch hand. But she had no idea how far down the wrong side of the tracks he'd lived. He'd learned at an early age that his background was socially unacceptable. He was so accustomed to hiding it that he had no idea where to begin discussing it now.

He pushed off the mantel and turned to face her. "You think I'm overly ambitious, and in some ways I am. I have a driving ambition not to ever again worry about being evicted or having the electricity turned off. I'm ambitious to never again water down a can of soup so it can be stretched for two meals because the pantry's empty and the month has thirty-one days in it. When I have a family, it'll be an overriding ambition of mine to make sure my kids don't have to wear the same pair of dirty jeans to school day in and day out because I can't afford to buy them new clothes and no one has the time or inclination to go to a Laundromat."

Her anger was gone, replaced by shock. Her hand flew to her mouth. "Oh, Stone. Was it that bad?"

A muscle worked in his jaw. "It was worse. The back problems that prevented my father from holding down a job had more to do with the fact he didn't have a backbone than with any physical ailment. The truth is he was a drinker and a gambler. My mother worked two and sometimes three jobs to support us, only to have him lose her earnings at the racetrack or the poker table. And every time it looked like things were getting better, they just got worse.''

He raked a hand through his hair. ''When I was eight, my father went on the wagon for a while, and things started looking up. We moved to an apartment where I had my own room, and my mother went out and got some rent-to-own bedroom furniture for it. Nothing fancy, but boy, I was proud of it. It was the first time I'd ever had a bed instead of just a mattress on the floor. I even got up the nerve to invite some friends home from school. It was the first time I'd ever had any friends over.''

He looked at Jamie. ''Well, my friends and I walked in just as the furniture people were repossessing my bedroom stuff. My father was there, soused to the gills, ranting and raving at the movers, making all kinds of wild promises to me. He always made promises he couldn't keep—clothes, shoes, Disneyland, toys. Good times were always just around the corner, always just one lucky bet away.

''God, I hated those promises. I still hate promises.'' His eyes pierced her soul. ''Never heard one yet that wasn't eventually broken.''

Did he mean their wedding vows? Tears sprang to Jamie's eyes and her mouth opened, her lips trembling.

How could she have been married to this man and never known this about him?

''I made up my mind, then and there, that when I grew up, I'd never be poor again. And I vowed that my word would mean something.''

She reached out and rested a quivering hand on his cheek, wishing she could somehow reach back in time and be there for him when the people who should have been weren't.

Tears muddled her vision her as she gazed into his eyes.

For just a second they were the eyes of a disappointed, disillusioned young boy—a boy who had somehow risen above his circumstances, who'd managed to work his way through college and up the ladder. With nothing but an example of what *not* to do, he'd achieved the kind of success most men only dream about.

But Stone didn't know he'd already achieved it. He was still struggling, still trying to prove himself.

Her mind raced. So many things looked different in light of this information. He wasn't driven by personal ambition—he was afraid of being like his father. He hadn't loved success more than her—he'd feared failure.

"Why didn't you tell me?" she whispered.

He lifted a shoulder. "Probably the same reason you didn't tell me about your stuttering."

Her heart slammed against her ribs. They'd been married, but in many ways, they'd been strangers. Both afraid to really trust the other, to let the other see their flaws, they'd let their marriage become a casualty of lonely secrets and private fears.

She gazed up to find him searching her face. His eyes were dark and penetrating, the edges etched with fine lines of pain.

"Oh, Stone," she breathed, moving toward him. "I never knew."

He grasped her upper arms and hauled her against his chest. She wound her arms around him and embraced him with all her might, burying her face in his neck.

They clung together, supported by each other's arms, the hug encompassing all they could not say. Regret. Forgiveness. And something deeper, something more profound, something her mind deliberately skirted, something she was afraid to confront and didn't have the nerve to name.

Stone's head dipped as she raised her face. His lips were hard and hungry, but as he drew back from the kiss, his eyes were soft and filled with something she'd never seen before.

Need. *He needed her.*

In all their time together, it was the first time she'd ever felt that. It strummed a soft chord in her heart, a chord that resonated throughout her mind and body and sent her blood singing through her veins. He'd often made her feel desired, but never really needed. Never as though she alone possessed something that could soothe his soul, something his heart was thirsting for.

She felt it now. He needed her acceptance, her understanding. Just as she'd needed it from him that afternoon. He'd given it to her freely, and her heart ached to do the same.

To do even more.

She gazed up at him, her throat constricted with emotion, her lips swollen and warm from his kiss, and felt as though the earth shifted and moved under her feet, tilting her toward him. She gazed into his dark eyes, feeling closer to him than she'd ever felt when they'd actually been married.

There was only one way to respond to his need—with a need of her own. Her fingers tightened on his shoulders. "I want to make love with you," she whispered. His five-o'clock shadow rasped her palm as her hands slid to his face, urging his mouth down.

He groaned and tightened his hold on her, his lips laying siege to hers. In another second he'd swung her legs out from under her and picked her up. Cradling her against his chest, one arm under her knees, he carried her down the hallway.

He nudged the bedroom door open with his foot, crossed the room and gently laid her on the quilt-topped bed.

Leaning over, he reclaimed her lips. A shiver of pleasure raced through her as his hands skimmed down her body. Gently, slowly, his fingers freed the buttons of her blouse. Pushing the chambray fabric out of his way, he ran a tantalizing finger down her cleavage, then unlatched the front hook of her bra.

Her breath caught in her throat. With tremulous hands, she reached up and unbuttoned his shirt. He shrugged out of it as her fingers feathered across his familiar chest, reveling in the hard muscle, the crisp hair, the solid, masculine feel of his flesh. The dim light spilling from the hallway revealed him just as she remembered—strong, manly, magnificent.

Memories flew through her mind like doves against the night sky—memories of other nights, of other times they'd made love. He'd always been an exquisite lover—sensitive, almost psychic, anticipating what she wanted before she knew herself. Desire, hot and liquid, flowed through her. Her fingers followed the path of dark hair down his hard stomach toward the proof of his own passion.

He kissed her again as he cupped her breasts in his large hands, his thumbs playing over the pebbled tips. Slowly, slowly his lips trailed down her throat to her chest, lingering at the rise of her breast, his tongue drawing languorous circles of excruciating pleasure.

He closed his warm mouth around a taut peak just as she thought she would die if he didn't. She arched against him and threaded her fingers through his thick hair, giving herself over to pure sensation.

Oh, God, she'd missed this. Not just the pleasure, but the closeness, the sharing, the sense of being a gift given, a gift received. She strained toward him, reaching for his belt buckle, longing to do away with all barriers between them.

She was jolted when he abruptly rolled away from her.

"Honey, I'd better go." His voice was low and husky, his breathing harsh.

"You don't want me?" Her voice was a broken whisper.

Didn't want her? Dear Lord, how could she think that? He looked down at her, her hair streaming out across the pillow, her eyes round and confused and hurt. It was precisely because he *did* want her so that he was leaving. His feelings for her were deep and tender and protective, and as much as it was killing him, he didn't want to do anything that would hurt her. If he made love to her now, before they settled their future, he feared that he'd do just that.

She wasn't the kind of woman who took lovemaking lightly. He needed to offer her more than a night of passion.

"Honey, I've never wanted anything more." His voice was as rough as gravel. "But I don't want to do something that's going to leave you full of regrets, and I don't want you avoiding me at the station."

He smoothed a strand of hair away from her troubled eyes. "Can you look me in the eye and tell me you're one-hundred-percent sure you'll have no regrets in the morning if we make love tonight?"

A shadow flickered across her face and she looked away. She was only confirming what he already knew, but disappointment drummed in his chest, anyway.

"That's what I thought." Stone swung his legs to the side of the bed and hauled himself upright. She stared down at the quilt and plucked at a thread as he reached for his shirt. "It's okay, Jamie. Sex was one of our biggest problems, anyway."

Her head jerked up and she stared at him, stricken. "It wasn't good for you?" she whispered.

If it had been any better, she would have driven him blind. He gave a slight smile as he reached out and ran a finger down her petal-soft cheek. "It was *too* good, honey. It overshadowed everything else. It prevented us from getting intimate in other ways—ways we're only now discovering." His fingers moved to her hair. The low, rumbly timbre of his voice betrayed the emotion that threatened to choke him. "Lord knows I want you, Jamie. But not just for a night. So as much as it's killing me, I'd better go."

He buttoned his shirt and stood. His eyes roved over her lush curves and he hesitated, wondering if he was in his right mind, knowing he was going to spend the rest of the night regretting this decision. Looking at her now, his resolve was already weakening. "And I'd better do it right now, honey, or I'll never make it out the door."

Chapter Nine

Jamie pulled a manila file from her desk drawer, her gaze again drifting across the newsroom to the closed door of Stone's office. He'd been holed up in there all morning, and she wondered what he was doing.

She couldn't get him off her mind. She wondered what he was wearing, what he'd had for breakfast, what he was thinking and most of all, how things really stood between them.

Annoyed with herself, she flipped open the file and pulled out a list of potential sites for the children's series. She had better things to do than moon over Stone like a teenaged groupie. But her mind refused to focus on the task before her, drawn instead to thoughts of Stone and his abrupt departure the night before.

She wished she knew why he'd left. When he'd said he didn't want her just for a night, did he mean he wanted her back for good, or was he just letting her down easy because he realized it would be a mistake to get involved again when he knew he would soon be leaving?

She'd spent the better part of the night weighing the question and she still didn't know. The only thing she knew for sure was that he'd warned her she would regret it if they made love, but he'd neglected to warn her how much she'd regret it if they didn't.

His sudden departure had left her as cold and lonely as her empty bed. She'd huddled under the covers and listened to the echo of his solid footsteps receding down the hall, to the creak of her front door opening, to the quiet thud of it closing behind him. She'd sobbed into her pillow until she'd cried all the tears she should have cried three years ago, when she hadn't let herself mourn the end of her marriage.

When she was finally spent and exhausted and certain no more tears could flow, she'd gotten up to lock the door and turn off the lights, only to discover he'd done it for her. The small, thoughtful gesture had started the tears anew. She'd slid to the floor and sat with her back against the door, bawling like a motherless calf until she finally dragged herself to the sofa for the rest of the restless night.

She was being ridiculous, she told herself. She should thank her lucky stars Stone had stopped things before they'd gone too far, whatever his reasons might have been. She had no business getting involved with him again, regardless of what intimacies they'd shared or what new insights she had into what made him tick or how deeply she still cared about him.

She gazed down at the file and sighed. Understanding him didn't change him. His motivations might be different from her father's, but the results were the same. Stone would still spend his life moving from place to place, putting his work ahead of everyone and everything else. And her priorities were still a home, roots, a family.

They were poles apart on what they wanted from life. She should be grateful he'd left last night, grateful he hadn't taken her up on her invitation. It was for the best.

So why did she feel so empty, as though she had nothing but a hole where her heart should be?

"How'd it go?"

Startled, Jamie looked up to see Todd standing beside

her desk. A wave of uneasiness flushed over her, and she rapidly shifted mental gears.

Oh, mercy. Why had she mentioned the series to him before she'd checked with Stone? It had been unfair of her to raise his hopes. And she wouldn't have, except she'd been so sure she could get him on as the reporter.

She swiveled her chair around to face him, desperately trying to think of a way to soften the news and coming up blank. "Not well, Todd," she finally admitted. "I'm afraid Mr. Milton has a preconceived notion of who should be the series reporter."

"And who's that?"

Oh, how had she gotten herself in this mess? She winced: "I hate to tell you this, but it's me."

His face grew red and his lips tightened into a hard line. "Well, well, well. Isn't that convenient?"

Jamie's fingers fidgeted with a pen. "Actually, it's not. I really wanted you to do it."

"Sure, Jamie, sure." Todd's pale blue eyes glittered hotly. "Don't expect me to buy that. Milton thinks you're the goose that laid the golden egg around here. He and that consultant will do anything you say to keep you happy."

"It's not that way, Todd."

"What's not what way?"

Jamie started at the sound of Stone's voice, as surprised at his steely tone as she was at his presence in the newsroom. She whipped her head around to find him standing at the opposite side of her desk, fixing Todd with a cold, suspicious glare.

"Stone." A flush spread guiltily up her neck. This was all her fault. She'd been out of line mentioning the series to Todd, and she didn't want him to get in further trouble now.

"What's not what way?" Stone repeated.

"The, um, new Piggly Wiggly store. Todd asked if it was north on First Street. But it's the other way. It's south."

"Piggly Wiggly, hmm?" Stone's narrowed eyes were as

skeptical as his tone, his gaze still locked on Todd. He was clearly not buying it. Jamie swallowed. Todd mustered a weak smile, waved at someone across the room and darted off on an imaginary mission.

Stone turned his gaze on Jamie, and her heart quickened. He gave a faint smile. "You would have been more believable if you'd said you were giving him directions to a liquor store."

He wasn't fooled, but he wasn't going to give her a hard time over it. Grateful, Jamie lifted her shoulders in a sheepish shrug.

Stone's brow furrowed into a concerned frown. "I don't like that guy, Jamie, and I don't trust him any further than I can kick a cow. I know you have a soft spot for children and pets, but Todd is neither. He worries me."

"He's just having a hard time accepting the fact he's been demoted. He'll get over it."

Stone shook his head. "It's not looking like it. He's not working out in the reporter pool. He's got a bad attitude, he argues with the assignment editors, and his stories stink. I've already spoken to Mr. Milton about him. We're going to transfer him to the promotions department, and if he can't cut it there, he's out the door." Stone lowered himself onto the corner of Jamie's desk, his knees nearly touching her forearm. "Unless I miss my guess, you've been carrying his weight around here for a long time."

Unable to deny it and disconcerted by his nearness, Jamie studied the end of her pen.

"You can't save him," Stone said softly. "I know from personal experience. He has to want to save himself."

Stone shifted his knee, and it accidently brushed her arm, sending shock waves vibrating through her. There was no such thing as casual contact with this man, she thought with chagrin. Especially after last night.

She realized she was staring at his leg, which suddenly struck her as a frankly sensuous body part. She glanced up, only to discover his eyes were even more dangerous territory, and quickly averted her gaze back to her pen.

Mercy. Her mouth was dry as the Sahara, her thoughts were scattered to the four winds, and he was looking at her, waiting for a response. She swallowed. "Did you want to see me about something?"

"Actually, I just wanted to see you."

His eyes caught hers and threw sparks like a blowtorch, making Jamie's breath catch in her chest.

The force of the attraction between them was enough to damn near knock him off the desk, Stone thought as he looked at her. He watched two pink patches form on her cheek, his heart turning over. He started to reach out and touch one of the blazing spots, then remembered they were in the middle of the newsroom.

Lord, she was lovely. It had taken every ounce of his self-control to leave her last night, and her face had haunted him all night long. Judging from the faint blue smudges under her eyes, she'd had a rough night, too.

"Do you want to come in my office and have some coffee?" he asked. "You look kind of beat."

"No. I'm fine." Her voice was a little too bright.

"How did you sleep last night?"

"Like a baby."

Stone shot her a grin. "Me, too. Every two hours I woke up and cried."

She laughed, and the sounded rippled through him, warming his chest like whiskey. He rubbed the spot with his hand.

He'd spent the entire night trying to come up with a way of winning her back. He knew his only hope lay in making a major career change. It had to be something that would allow him to stay in one place, that would let him use his skills and experience, that would keep him challenged. He knew himself well enough to know that anything less would make him miserable—and if he were miserable, he'd ultimately make Jamie unhappy, too.

As the dawn light had filtered through the drapes of his hotel room window, he'd finally hit on an idea, and he'd spent the morning putting it into action.

It was a risk—an enormous one. If he failed, he could endanger his reputation as a consultant, and his whole business could crumple at his feet. Even if he succeeded, he had no guarantee Jamie would give him another chance.

He looked at her now, at her blond hair shining like polished pine, at her wide, pansy blue eyes trying to avoid making contact with his, and an aching emptiness spread through his middle, an emptiness the vending machine sandwich he'd eaten at his desk couldn't fill. He wanted her back, not just for a night, but for the rest his life. If there was a chance he could have her, it was worth any risk he had to take.

"I couldn't get you off my mind all night."

"What were you thinking?" Her voice sounded slightly off-key.

He was tempted to tell her, but it was too soon. Too many factors were beyond his control, and he had no guarantee things would work out as he hoped. He made a point of never promising things he wasn't sure he could deliver.

Action was the only thing that counted. He'd explain it all later, if and when he had solid results to show her.

He gave her a smile. "I was thinking I'd like to spend a day with you someplace besides here. What are you doing on Saturday?"

She clasped her chest, feigning a heart attack. "Don't tell me you're actually taking a day off."

"I am. And I'd like to spend it with you."

"I can't. I've made plans to scout some locations for the children's series. The fire station, the skating rink and the municipal park."

"Sounds like fun."

Her mouth curved into an oblique smile. "Sorry, Stone. I've already got a date."

His stomach knotted. "Who the hell with?"

"Michael."

She couldn't have looked more like a cat who'd swallowed a canary unless she'd had tail feathers coming out of her mouth, Stone thought darkly. His eyebrows drew together in a scowl. "And just who in blue blazes is that?"

She inclined her head and gave him a Cheshire Cat grin, pausing melodramatically. "The boy from the children's home. I thought it might be a good idea to get a child's point of view, so I made arrangements for him to spend the day with me."

For a moment there, she'd really had him going. He'd never felt jealousy like that before; his veins were flooded with adrenaline, and the force of it made his head reel. He reached up and rubbed the back of his neck, mustering a wan smile and trying his darnedest to appear nonchalant. "Mind if I tag along?"

Jamie gazed up at him, her expression guarded. "I don't know if it's a good idea."

"Why not? Michael could probably benefit from some masculine companionship."

She paused. Her hesitation told him he'd plucked a heart-string, and he mercilessly pressed his advantage.

"We'll have a pint-size chaperon along in case you're worried you can't restrain yourself around me," he said, baiting her wickedly.

Her spine shot up like an arrow and her expression grew indignant. "That's the least of my concerns!"

"Good." He hoisted himself off her desk and flashed a grin. "I'll pick you up at nine."

Stone knotted the string on the bright yellow kite and handed it to Michael. "All set and ready for a test flight."

"Oh, boy!" Michael sprang to his feet, his eyes bright and animated.

Stone unfolded his legs and rose from the faded quilt. "Come on. I'll help you launch it." He grinned at Jamie. "Want to copilot?"

She shook her head, returning his smile. "I'll play mission control. That way I can stay right here and soak up some sunshine."

She leaned back on her elbows and watched them walk

to a clearing along Fairfield Lake, Stone's hand on the boy's shoulder. Anyone seeing them together would probably think they were father and son, she thought.

The thought sent a pang through her chest. She'd never seen Stone one-on-one with a child before, and she'd been surprised at how easily he'd developed a rapport with Michael. Stone's jokes and gentle horseplay had managed to bring the six-year-old out of his shell during their morning at the local fire station, where they'd toured the firemen's quarters, slid down the pole and climbed aboard a fire truck. After the first few minutes with Stone, Michael had hardly stuttered at all.

Jamie glanced at the pile of chicken bones heaped in Michael's empty fast-food box and smiled. If his appetite were any indication, he was having a great time.

And so was she, she thought with a contented sigh. She stretched out on the blanket and turned her face to the sun, savoring the unseasonably warm weather, letting the warm rays thaw the winter out of her body.

Which was exactly what Stone was doing to her heart. Feelings she'd thought dead and gone had only been in hibernation, and she could no more stop them from blooming inside her than the oaks overhead could resist budding in the sun.

She watched him in the distance as he held the kite aloft while Michael ran along the shore. The string pulled taut and a gust of wind yanked it skyward. Michael let out a squeal of delight. Stone's deep, hearty laughter mingled with it and drifted to Jamie on the breeze as the kite soared higher. Stone turned and smiled at her, and her heart warmed another degree as it, too, lifted skyward.

Stone gave Michael two thumbs up, then jogged back to join her. Her pulse sped as he lowered himself beside her on the blanket. "You're pretty handy with a kite," she remarked.

"Beginner's luck." His arm brushed hers as he stretched out his legs and a current of electricity scurried along her skin. "That's the first time I've ever done it."

Jamie's eyebrows rose. "You've never flown a kite before?"

"Never." His eyes were more gold than brown in the sunshine. "But then, this is the first time I've ever spent any time in a park. For that matter, if you don't count business functions, this is the first time I've ever been on a picnic, either."

She stared at him, sifting out the implications behind his words. Stone's parents had never bought him a kite, never taken him to a park, never gone on a family picnic?

How could she have been married to this man and never realized that before? The things he was telling her added up to a childhood that was as deprived emotionally as it had been materially.

Jamie's heart ached for him. Her father might have been distant and critical, but she'd been blessed with loving attention from her mother and grandmother.

For all practical purposes, Stone had had no one. The fact he'd grown up to be a kind, decent man in spite of it all was nothing short of a miracle.

Jamie placed her hand on his arm and gave him a soft smile. "I never would have guessed. You looked like an old hand."

Stone's lips curved into a grin, but his eyes held no sign of mirth. "When you come from a background like mine, you learn to look like you know what you're doing whether you really do or not. The kite was easy. It came with directions." He rolled over, propped himself on an elbow and lightly touched the tip of her nose. "You, on the other hand, did not."

He was so close she could see the golden facets in his eyes and smell his clean, masculine scent. "What instructions would you have wanted?"

He gave her a rakish grin. "'This end up' would have been nice."

Jamie laughed and pushed his chest hard enough to roll him on his back. "You never had a problem figuring that part out." She grinned down at him. "You're incorrigible, Stone."

His arm snaked out and grabbed her around the waist. He hoisted her on top of him. "And you're irresistible."

He held her tight against him, one hand low on her hip, the other high on her back. They were chest to chest, belly to belly, heartbeat to heartbeat, and her laughter faded as the heat of his body crept through her clothing and became her own. She raised her head and looked at him. His eyes were dark and wanting, his mouth a slightly parted invitation. Desire, hot and urgent, pulsed through her. Her lips lowered as if of their own volition.

The contact of his mouth on hers was like a match tossed into a firecracker factory. The force of it frightened her. Her reaction was so strong, the pull so powerful, she was afraid she'd lose all control, all decorum, all touch with reality.

Shaken, she rolled away and sat up. "We need to keep an eye on Michael," she murmured, her voice as thin and breathless as high-altitude air.

Stone looked over his shoulder at the boy, who was merrily feeding line to the kite. "Right," he said with a sigh, hauling himself upright.

She straightened her sweater, wishing she could straighten her emotions as easily, and tried to recapture some sense of sanity by recalling what they'd been talking about. "I believe you were telling me something about instructions."

He stretched his long, jeans-clad legs and leaned back on his elbows, gazing at the tight, heavy blossoms on a nearby dogwood. "I wish I'd had instructions on how to make you happy when we were married." He gazed at her, his eyes dark and serious. "Now I wish I had instructions on how to start all over."

Her heart pounded against her rib cage. He leaned forward, reached out a hand and softly traced the curve of her cheek, his eyes lit with something that made her chest ache and her throat tighten. "Jamie, I want you to know I'm working on a major career change. I'm not sure if it's going to work out yet, so I won't get into the details, but I want you to know I'm trying to change."

She nodded, her heart filled with unanswered questions.

"As for starting over... Do I have a chance, Jamie?"

Before she could answer, a loud, plaintive wail cut the air. Alarmed, Jamie snapped her head around, looking for Michael. By the time she caught sight of his distorted, tear-streaked face, Stone was already on his feet, racing toward him. Jamie scrambled after him, frantic with worry.

Stone was holding the child in his arms as she pulled up beside them. "He's not hurt," he reassured her.

"What happened?"

"It c-c-c-crashed!" Sobbing, the boy pointed to the top of a tree, where a slash of yellow dangled among the budding branches.

Stone's large hand patted the boy's back. "It's all right, little buddy. We'll get it down."

"I—I didn't m-m-mean t-t-to d-d-do it," the boy stammered.

Stone ruffled his hair. "I know. No one's mad at you."

Mad? Jamie glanced at Stone. Why would he say an odd thing like that?

Her gaze darted to the boy as Stone set him on his feet. She was shocked to note how rigidly he held himself, almost as if he expected a blow. The look on his face was one of pure terror as he tearfully looked from Jamie to Stone.

"Are y-you g-g-going to punish m-m-me?"

Who on earth would punish a youngster for accidentally wrecking a kite? Someone from Michael's past, she realized with a shock. And whoever it was, their idea of punishment was enough to make the boy tremble.

Stone crouched beside the child and put an arm around him. "Of course not. You didn't do anything wrong."

Jamie watched the child's fear subside as Stone talked quietly to him, her shock giving way to anger. How could anyone treat a child so harshly that he was terrified of making a minor mistake? No telling what the boy had experienced before he'd arrived at the children's home.

No telling what Stone had experienced as a child, either, she thought suddenly. He'd been immediately attuned to the boy's emotions.

Her heart filled with tenderness as she watched Stone straighten up and hold out his hand to the boy. "Come on, sport. Let's go tug on the line and see if we can get it loose."

The child wiped his eyes on his shirtsleeve and nodded. Stone smiled, and the boy placed his small hand in Stone's outstretched one. Together they walked toward the tree.

Jamie wiped her own eyes as she watched them, her mind ringing with his question.

Could she give Stone another chance?

The more she saw him, the more time they spent together, the more she opened up to him and felt him opening up to her, the more she realized how deep her feelings for him ran.

Could she give him another chance, knowing full well that life with Stone meant a lifetime of playing second fiddle to his work—a lifetime of lonely nights and solitary weekends, of harried mornings and cold dinners, of frequent moves, of her own career floundering or completely disappearing? Could she do it, knowing how hard it was to raise a family under those circumstances?

He'd said he was adjusting his career. Did he mean he was trying to change? Would he? *Could* he?

And if he couldn't, could she?

The afternoon sun hovered low in the sky as Stone walked Jamie down the broad steps of the children's home toward the parking lot. They'd left Michael in the central playroom, excitedly recounting his day and proudly displaying the recovered kite to his friends.

"I think Michael had a great time today," Jamie remarked.

Stone nodded, swallowing around the lump in his throat

that had inexplicably formed as they'd walked away from the boy. The kid had really gotten to him. Something in his chest had just kind of melted when the little guy had thrown those scrawny freckled arms around his neck and hugged him goodbye. Despite Michael's upbeat mood, Stone had hated leaving him inside the huge, impersonal building in the care of paid staff. A child like that deserved a real home and a real family.

The kind he used to imagine having himself, Stone thought. As a boy, he'd invented an entire imaginary family, and he'd thought about them so often and so intensely that they'd almost seemed real. His fantasy mom had smiled and laughed a lot, and she was always home at night to tuck him into his own bed. His imaginary dad had picked him up on his shoulders and pitched softball with him and always kept his promises. They'd lived in a make-believe house that had a real backyard and a pantry that was always full.

Food. Shelter. Love. It was a crime that any child would be denied things as basic as the stuff of his boyhood dreams. The same stuff Michael no doubt dreamed about now.

Especially love. From the few hours he'd spent with Michael, he could tell that was what the boy craved most of all. The need had really touched Stone's heart, because it was the one thing he still longed for, too.

A great, yawning hunger gnawed at his belly as he sneaked a glance at Jamie. She'd offered him love once, and he'd let it slip through his fingers. He'd felt love from her, he'd felt love for her, but he hadn't known how to handle it, hadn't known how to make her happy.

Did he have the ability to give her all that she deserved, all that she needed? Maybe he was too old to learn how. Maybe he was only kidding himself, pretending that he could. Maybe he would only end up hurting her again.

The thought made his stomach tighten. He hadn't realized how badly he'd hurt her in their marriage, and he'd rather cut off his right arm than ever do that again.

"Are you all right?" she asked. "You seem kind of pensive."

He unlocked the Jeep, opened her door and sidestepped the question. "I'm fine. I was just thinking about Michael."

Jamie seated herself and looked up at him, her eyes the same shade of dark blue as the twilight sky. "He's terrific, isn't he? Being with him today makes me wish..."

She looked away, but not before Stone caught the wistful look in her eyes.

"Wish what?"

She gave a small sigh. "That I could take him home and love him and make him forget everything bad that's ever happened to him. If I didn't think he'd be better with off with a two-parent family, I think I'd try to adopt him myself."

The lump in Stone's throat grew into the size of a boulder. He circled the car and climbed in. "You're doing a terrific thing for him, trying to find him a home."

"I just hope it works." Her hand brushed his as she fastened her seat belt. "He needs a male figure in his life. He really seemed to relate to you today."

Stone shrugged. "I think we have a lot in common." *Too much,* he added silently, thinking of his own dismal childhood.

Jamie nodded, her eyes somber, and he knew she was thinking the same thing. He was grateful she understood him well enough not to press for details, to let him tell her about his past in his own way and at his own pace.

"He needs someone like you," she said softly. "It was wonderful of you to offer to take him fishing next weekend."

If he didn't lighten up and get her to do the same, he was going to ruin a perfect day. He forced a smile. "Yeah, well, I'm looking forward to it. It'll be fun watching you bait the hooks."

"Bait hooks?" She stared at him, her eyes wide. He could tell the exact moment she realized he was teasing. She wagged a finger at him. "Whoa, there, Johnson! No

one said anything about me coming along, much less baiting hooks.''

His grin broadened. "All right. You don't have to pull
worm duty. But you do want to come, don't you?"

"Only if you promise to use plastic lures."

"It's a deal." Stone turned the key in the ignition, inordinately pleased to have so easily arranged another date
with her. "You know, I had more fun today than I've had
in a long, long time. How about you?"

"I hate to see the day end," she admitted.

His sentiments exactly. He didn't want to be alone. Because when he was, he was going to have to give some
serious thought to what the hell he was doing.

What right did he have to be insinuating his way back
into her life? What did he have to offer her? He was trying
to improve his work situation, but that was just an external
problem.

A bigger, deeper question lay at the core of their relationship: did he have the ability to love Jamie like she
needed to be loved?

Time enough to deal with that later, he thought, deliberately shoving the thought aside.

"No reason to end the day yet," he said as he backed
the vehicle out of the parking slot. "Why don't we stop at
a grocery store, grab some provisions and let me borrow
your kitchen? I'm sick to death of restaurant food and have
a powerful urge to bang around some pans."

Jamie grinned. "You're on."

Thirty minutes later they were cruising the aisles at Safe-
way. It was like old times, and the sheer ordinariness of it
thrilled her. Passing avocadoes back and forth for a test
squeeze, conferring over the meat counter, comparing notes
at the spice display seemed as special an event as the Arts
Ball.

At the checkout stand, Jamie picked up a tabloid newspaper and showed it to Stone. "Look at this headline—
'Alien Babies Found in Wheat Fields.'" She gave him a

teasing grin. "If you call the station now, there's still time to put the story on the ten-o'clock news."

Stone's smile was warm, but his eyes were warmer. "I don't care if alien babies eat their way through our dinner rolls, I'm not calling the station tonight. I'm off duty."

Off duty. Never had she heard Stone say such a thing. She hadn't known he was capable of saying those words in the same sentence, much less together.

He's trying, she thought. *He's really trying.* The thought made her hand tremble as she placed the tabloid back in the wire rack while he paid for the groceries.

They loaded the car, drove to Jamie's house and toted in the bags, moving in an easy, harmonious ballet.

Just like an old married couple. Jamie froze in the middle of unpacking a grocery sack, a package of cheese in her hand. If they hadn't divorced, that's what they'd be by now. Would they be parents, too? It had felt wonderful today, spending time with Stone and Michael. It had been easy to fantasize that they were a real family.

A jolt of pain raced through her, and she deliberately pushed away the thought. She didn't want to think about "what ifs" tonight. She wanted to stay in the here and now, to enjoy the present, to be caught up in the moment.

She opened the refrigerator to put away the cheese. "When are you going to tell me what you're cooking?"

"As soon as I figure it out." Stone rummaged in a bottom cabinet until he located a baking dish. "Trust me. I have a concept."

It was the favorite saying of a producer they'd worked with in Tulsa, a person notorious for half-baked ideas that invariably flopped, and the old memory made Jamie laugh. "Maybe I should order a pizza as a back-up."

"O ye of little faith," Stone scolded, plopping a piece of chicken in the dish.

Maybe she was, Jamie reflected. His actions today indicated he was trying to change. Maybe she should give him the benefit of the doubt.

She gave him a smile, the corners of her lips wobbling

a bit from suppressed emotion. She did her best to sound lighthearted and chipper. "I do have faith in you, Stone. How can I help make your concept a reality?"

He looked at her, a chicken breast dangling from his hand, his eyes no longer laughing. He hesitated just a heartbeat, just long enough to make her think he was going to answer her thoughts. Then his dimple flashed.

"I could use a good sous-chef. Can you make a salad?"

It was like old times, only better, Stone thought. They joked and reminisced, and he made Jamie laugh at newsroom anecdotes until she'd nearly blown out the candle he'd lit in the center of the table. Lord, he loved making her laugh—and he loved watching her eat something he'd cooked for her. He wasn't sure if the food was actually as good as he thought it was, or if it just seemed that way because he was sitting beside her at her small, round kitchen table.

She put down her fork and sighed contentedly. "That was wonderful. What do you call that dish?"

He watched the candlelight flicker across her soft features and felt his heart lurch in his chest. All of his resolve from the other night, all of his intentions to keep his distance, all of his doubts about whether or not he was good for her were forgotten. He only remembered the softness of her lips, the texture of her skin, the responsiveness of her body. He wanted her, and he answered instinctively.

"Seduction chicken." His voice came out low and smoky, and the air in the room suddenly seemed the same way—somehow heavier and harder to breathe. His hand stretched out and covered hers. "So tell me, Jamie. Did it work?"

Her other hand fluttered to her chest, and he heard the sharp intake of her breath. She averted her eyes. "I thought we were going to keep things simple," she mumbled.

Damn it, she was right—but his feelings for her weren't simple at all. Tier upon tier of complex, intertwined emotions swirled through him like the complicated, changing designs of a kaleidoscope.

A frustrated sigh hissed through his teeth. He needed to get out of here before he said or did something he'd regret.

"Right." He released her hand, scooted back his chair and attempted a smile. "I'll tackle the dishes if you'll deal with the leftovers. How's that for simple?"

They worked together smoothly enough, but the easy rapport was gone, replaced with a thick cord of tension that vibrated in the air between them.

He poured dry soap into the dishwasher, switched it on and straightened. "Well, that's a wrap." He watched her drape a kitchen towel across the oven handle and pushed himself off the kitchen counter. "I think we'd better wrap up the evening, too."

She walked with him to the foyer. The warm, feather-soft weight of her hand settled on his arm as he reached for the doorknob. "Thanks for coming today. Michael really enjoyed your company."

"And you?"

She nodded. "Me, too." She tilted her head as she gazed up at him. "You know, I'd never seen you with a child before. You're terrific with kids."

He'd thought the same thing of her, but what would be the point of saying it? It would just raise issues he wasn't ready to address. Probably had no business addressing. The career change he was trying to make was a long shot at best. It would be cruel to tell her about it, to lead her on, to persuade her they could have a future together only to have it all fall through.

It might be even crueler to have it all work out, Stone thought grimly. Because as much as he hated to acknowledge it, he was deep-down afraid that their backgrounds were just too different for things to ever work out between them.

He wasn't the kind of man a woman like Jamie needed. She deserved someone who knew about marriage, who knew about families, who knew how to be a good parent.

He didn't know the first thing about any of that. If he were halfway decent, he'd get out of the picture and let her find someone who'd had some positive role models, whose upbringing was more like hers, who didn't have a track record of letting her down once before.

He raked his hand through his hair, knowing he wasn't that noble. At least not yet. He would only be at the station a few more weeks, and it might be all the time with her he'd ever get. He wanted to squeeze in every damn second he could, because the memories might have to last a lifetime.

If he didn't make love to her, he reasoned, he couldn't hurt her. If he could keep from acting on his constant, compelling urges to touch her, to hold her, to slowly remove her clothes and kiss every inch of her body, he could spend as much time with her as he wanted and not break her heart when his time at the station was over.

It was a deal with the devil himself, he thought dourly.

"Good night, Jamie." He pulled her to him, planted a soft, chaste kiss on her forehead, then dropped his arms and stepped out the door.

She followed him to the porch, her knees wobbly, her pulse thrumming, and watched him climb into his car. His restraint packed as much emotional wallop as his most passionate kisses. Her senses reeling, she watched until his taillights disappeared around the corner, then she went back inside and wandered aimlessly through her house.

She ended up in her bedroom, staring at the music box. She lifted the lid and let the familiar tune escape into the air. Memories swirled around her like the lilting notes, and when her gaze fell on the rocking chair in the corner, one memory reached out and grabbed her so hard that her breath caught in her throat.

In her mind's eye, she saw another rocking chair in another bedroom—the bedroom at a bed-and-breakfast where she and Stone had stayed on their honeymoon.

She closed her eyes, her hand on the dresser beside the

tiny spinning bride and groom, and let the memory wash over her.

They'd stepped out of the shower, their skin tingling from the hot, streaming water and even hotter kisses, and playfully toweled each other off. Stone had led her to the rocking chair and pulled her onto his lap.

She must have looked bewildered, because he'd given her a rakish grin. "Trust me. I've got a concept," he'd said then.

The memory made her bite her lip and smile.

He'd lifted her up and eased her down, then set the rocking chair in motion. It had been like flying, like being suspended in air, her only contact with gravity the delicious, mind-shattering contact with Stone. She'd ridden him as if he were Pegasus, a winged horse carrying her to the stars. Her pleasure had mounted like a cumulus cloud, building upon itself, layer upon layer, until it burst around her.

She'd called his name as he'd whispered hers, the exchange like the inhale-exhale of a single breath, and in that moment they were one. Complete. Replete. Whole.

And wholly married.

The memory was so sweet her heart throbbed like a sore tooth. Tears clouded her eyes. Could they ever have that again?

Could they have a marriage like that moment? Could they meet each other's needs that fully, be that open and trusting and loving?

With a shaky sigh, Jamie lowered herself into the rocking chair and stared at the spinning figures of the music box. It would kill her to become involved with Stone and have the relationship fail again. She didn't know if she dared to try.

She didn't know if she dared not to.

Ah, heck. Who was she trying to kid? Her heart had already made that decision. Despite all her efforts to the contrary, she'd fallen in love with her own ex-husband.

No. She'd never stopped loving him in the first place. *She still loved Stone.*

Now that she'd admitted it, what in the world was she going to do about it? The rocking chair creaked as she pushed her toe against the floor, hoping its soothing rhythm would calm her tumultuous thoughts.

Stone had said he was making changes in his career, but he hadn't given her any specifics. Jamie didn't doubt his good intentions, but she didn't know if he was capable of acting on them. His need to prove himself through success was too deeply ingrained. When the next offer came, he was likely to find himself unable to resist it.

Even worse, he might find he resented her for holding him back if he did.

She jerked the chair to a halt, crossed the room and flipped the lid on the music box, but the silence didn't quiet her mind. She stood by the bureau, her fingers on the box, and weighed her options.

She couldn't change Stone. The only person she could change was herself.

If their relationship was ever going to work, she'd have to accept life on his terms. That meant being content with a nomadic life-style, giving up her dream of a permanent home, being willing to cope with his long hours and erratic schedule. Could she do it?

How could she not? The alternative was a life without him, and anything was better than that. What good was a sense of permanence if it only meant a permanently empty heart?

She lifted her chin. She needed a new outlook. She would begin by trying to see things differently. She'd try to find a sense of adventure, she'd let go of old baggage, she'd focus on what she stood to gain, not what she stood to lose.

She'd give it a chance. She'd give *them* a chance. Because in the farthest corners of her heart she knew that this was her once-in-a-lifetime chance at love.

Chapter Ten

Jamie readjusted the tripod under her arm as she walked down the sun-dappled trail toward the riding stables at Fairfield Park, glad to be outdoors on such a beautiful afternoon. Overhanging tree limbs cast graceful, shifting shadows, azaleas blazed with brilliant fury, and the fresh, green scent of May filled the air. She inhaled appreciatively. "What a glorious day! Everything looks so bright and new and beautiful."

Harold hoisted the camera on his shoulder, adjusted the power pack below his potbelly and grinned, his weathered face creasing like the instep of an old shoe. "I gotta say, kiddo, bein' in love sure agrees with you."

Jamie gave a sheepish smile. It had rapidly spread through the station's grapevine that she and Stone had been seeing each other the past few weeks.

Not that they'd exactly tried to hide it. Stone took her to lunch nearly every day, often stopped by her desk in the newsroom and took her to dinner every evening.

They'd spent a lot of time with Michael, too. The three of them were together every weekend, tending the vegetable garden they'd planted in Jamie's backyard, visiting

Grams and finding ways to enjoy the beautiful spring weather.

The child had entirely captured Jamie's heart, and she was certain Stone felt the same way. The man and the boy seemed to bring out the best in each other. Michael's shyness disappeared when he was with Stone, and Stone was more patient and playful with the child than Jamie had ever seen him being. Watching them together, she found it easy to pretend the three of them were a real family, and doing so had become one of Jamie's favorite fantasies.

Her other fantasies all dealt exclusively with Stone. They'd continued to keep their sexual relationship on hold, limiting physical contact to end-of-the-evening kisses—kisses that left her burning for more. She knew it was wise to wait, that lovemaking was sure to complicate their relationship, that they still needed to settle the issues that had driven them apart, but she was growing unbearably frustrated all the same.

The attraction between them was hotter than ever. When Michael wasn't along, they spent their time in restaurants and movies and other public places, trying to keep the fire between them from blazing out of control.

Which was becoming more and more difficult. Sexual tension stretched between them like a rubber band about to snap. They'd given up dining at Jamie's house because saying good-night had become a test of self-control they'd both been about to flunk.

It was time to settle the question of their future.

Over the past few weeks, Jamie had pondered it long and hard. As she'd thought about their past together, she'd been forced to take a close look at her own role in their marriage, and she'd come to realize she wasn't entirely blameless.

She'd been as trapped by her past as Stone was by his. She'd thought she was unlovable if she didn't measure up to some impossible ideal of perfection, and she'd been applying an equally impossible ideal of perfection to her concept of a stable marriage.

She'd always thought stability meant living in one place.

But she'd recently come to realize it meant loving a man like Stone—a man as steady as a rock, a man whose character was as solid as his name.

She'd been wrong to think home was a place. Home was where the heart was, and hers would always be with Stone.

He'd said he'd changed, she mused, and his behavior bore it out. He still worked long hours, but he left the stacks of paperwork that used to eat up all his free time at the office. When he was with her, he was completely there—attentive, interested, fully present.

Everything was perfect, except for one little, niggling thing: Stone hadn't exactly said he wanted to marry her again.

In fact, he hadn't even used the *L* word.

For that matter, he'd been unusually silent on the topic of how he felt about her or any plans for the future at all.

He was probably just waiting for the right time and place to bring up the topic, she rationalized. He hadn't said any more about making changes in his career, either, but she hadn't pressed him on it, figuring that whatever he'd been working on had fallen through. She'd reached the conclusion that loving Stone meant accepting him just as he was, and that meant accepting the fact that his drive to succeed was probably too much a part of him to ever be permanently altered.

Surely she could meet him halfway. If he would make her a priority in his life, she'd move with him wherever he wanted.

Which was why she'd sold her house. She'd listed it with a real estate agent two weeks ago, and the very first couple who'd seen it had offered her full list price.

She smiled, thinking how surprised Stone would be. He was due to leave this afternoon on a week-long business trip to the station's corporate headquarters in Chicago, and she planned to tell him when he returned. She knew how much he valued action over words. What better way to show him how much she loved him than to be ready to go with him when he left for his next assignment?

Her smile widened as she imagined the scenario. She would invite him to dinner and fix that delicious "Seduction Chicken" dish he'd prepared for her a few weeks ago. She'd wait for him on the front porch so she could see his face when he saw the "Sold" sign on her front lawn. He'd be shocked. His eyebrows would quirk upward in that adorable way of his, and he'd probably gesture to the sign as he asked what was going on. She'd put her arms around his broad back, pull him close and tell him she didn't want anything in her life that would keep her from being with him. She'd tell him she loved him more than anything in the world, that wherever he was, that was where she wanted to be. And then...

"Hand me that tripod, would you, kiddo?" Jamie had been so lost in her daydream she hadn't realized they'd already arrived at the riding stables, the taping site for this week's "Home of My Own" segment. Pulling her thoughts back to the present, she quickly passed the tripod to Harold and turned to watch the horses in the fenced corral.

A white-faced roan neighed and tossed his head, baring enormous yellow teeth in what looked like a goofy grin. Jamie laughed. That was what she felt like when she was sitting at the anchor desk, she thought. Being on the air no longer paralyzed her with fright, but she still felt thoroughly ridiculous.

Grams said it must not be her cup of tea. Harold said it wasn't her calling. All Jamie knew was that sitting in a spotlight and reading from a script seemed silly and vacant, especially compared to what she was accomplishing with the children's series.

A sense of satisfaction swelled within her at the thought of the series. It was going well—very well. The stories were turning out to be more effective than she'd ever imagined, exceeding her wildest hopes.

They'd aired four segments so far, and all of the children they'd featured had had multiple offers for adoption. Several couples were undergoing the screening process now. If everything went smoothly, the children would be placed in permanent homes in just a few months.

Harold looked up and scowled. "Uh-oh. Don't look now, but here comes the back half of a horse's anatomy."

Jamie turned to follow his gaze and saw an all-too-familiar figure walking toward her.

Todd. A knot of revulsion formed in Jamie's stomach at the sight of him. She'd managed to avoid him ever since he'd been transferred to the promotions department a few weeks ago. She was less than delighted to see him now, but she forced what she hoped was a pleasant expression on her face. "Hello, Todd. What brings you out here?"

The man's thin lips curled into a plastic smile. "I'm supposed to get footage for a promotional spot about you."

Jamie looked over his shoulder and saw a production photographer mounting his camera on a tripod. "Stone mentioned the promo, but I didn't know it was supposed to be shot today."

Todd shrugged. "For some reason, he insisted on using today's kid."

The soft spot Stone occupied in Jamie's heart warmed and expanded. The segment they were shooting today featured Michael. Stone knew that being highlighted in the promo meant the boy would get extra exposure, which might help him find a home.

"What are you going to shoot?" Jamie asked.

"Just some candids of you with the kid."

Her eyes fell to the stapled papers in his hand. "Can I look at the script?"

Todd shook his head. "Stone said it's supposed to be a surprise. He doesn't want you to see it."

"Why on earth not?"

He shrugged. "He said you'd want to tone down all the nice things it says about you."

Michael and Mrs. Mathis rounded the stables just then, and Jamie excused herself, glad to have a reason to end the conversation with the unpleasant man.

She greeted the child with a big hug as the social worker

waved and seated herself on a bench under a shade tree. "Are you excited about being on TV?" she asked the boy as he clung to her.

Michael gazed up with troubled hazel eyes, his arms still around her neck. "N-no. I'm scared."

Jamie immediately sensed the problem. She knelt beside him. "You don't have to talk unless you want to," she said gently.

"B-b-b-but one of m-my friends said I w-w-wouldn't find a home unless I t-t-talk. He said n-no one w-w-will w-w-want m-me."

Jamie gave him a squeeze. "That's not true."

"B-b-but I'll have a b-b-better chance if I t-t-talk, w-w-won't I?"

Jamie tried to choose her words carefully. "When you talk, you let people see how kind and bright you are. And if you talk during the story, they can see that your problem doesn't keep you from being able to communicate."

The dubious look on Michael's face tugged at her heart. She knew what he was thinking: that he was flawed and unlovable. She understood his anguish because she'd felt it herself.

Stone's acceptance of her problem had helped her to accept it, too. She longed to do the same for Michael. Maybe by sharing her experience, she could help him understand that stuttering didn't have to limit him.

She tightened her arm around him. "Remember I told you I used to stutter? Well, I'll tell you a secret—I'm still terrified of having it happen. And it's really silly, but t-t-talking about stuttering, t-t-elling people about it, makes me d-d-do it." Jamie felt her face flush. She forced a smile. "See? It's happening right n-now." She paused and drew a deep breath, reminding herself that allowing the boy to see that she shared his problem might help him find the self-acceptance he so desperately needed.

He looked at her with undisguised interest. "So how d-do you t-t-talk on T-TV?"

"I c-concentrate on what I'm talking about and try to

forget about myself." She smiled at him conspiratorially. "See? It's already working. And sometimes I picture people in their underwear."

Michael grinned, then burst into giggles.

"Your speech therapist will teach you lots of tricks."

Stone's consulting firm had paid for a year of therapy for the boy, and he was due to start his sessions next week. Jamie gave him a hug. "I'll tell you what. Let's concentrate on just having fun today. We'll use a boom mike to record everything we say, and if we have a good enough time, I bet we'll catch you talking without you even knowing it."

"I w-w-won't have t-to t-t-talk into a m-microphone?"

"No."

The boy gave a broad, gap-toothed grin. "All r-right!"

Jamie held her palms up. "Give me ten."

The boy slapped her hands heartily. She laughed and patted his back. "Why don't you go sit by Mrs. Mathis until we're ready to start? Then you and I will saddle up a couple of ponies and go for a ride."

"Cool!"

Jamie watched him run toward the social worker, then stepped back and bumped into something. Turning, she realized it was Todd. "Oh—sorry! I didn't know you were there."

"No problem." Todd gestured to the production photographer, who was shutting off a camera aimed right at Jamie. "We were just shooting some footage of your conversation with the kid."

Alarm raced through her. He'd evidently recorded the entire exchange. Was the camera within earshot? Had he been standing close enough to overhear her conversation with Michael?

Jamie felt her her face flush. It didn't matter, she told herself fiercely, fighting off the old feelings of shame. Todd was just shooting footage. The sound wouldn't be used in the finished spot.

Besides, what difference did it make if Todd knew she stuttered? It wouldn't be the end of the world if he knew she had a problem. Heaven only knew he had enough problems of his own.

"Hello," called a familiar voice.

Stone. Todd forgotten, her pulse quickened as she turned to see him sauntering up the trail behind her. Funny how just the sound of his voice could affect her heart rate, how the sight of him could brighten her day.

She hurried toward him. "What a surprise! I thought you were on your way to Chicago."

He pulled her to him for a quick kiss. "I decided to drop by and check on the promotion on my way to the airport. It seemed like a good excuse to see you one more time before I left."

He stepped back and squeezed her hands, his heart lurching at the way she smiled up at him. Damn it, he reproached himself, he needed to be distancing himself from her, not telling her how much he wanted to see her, but whenever he was around her, distance was the last thing he wanted to create.

He'd have to create some soon, he thought grimly. His plans to change his career were looking more and more like a lost cause. Unless he pulled off a major miracle in Chicago, he'd be heading off to his next consulting job in just two more weeks.

A surge of pain rushed through him at the thought. It was just as well he'd soon be leaving, he thought bleakly. He had nothing to offer her—nothing she really needed. He'd grown to realize that, as he'd watched her with Michael over the past month. What Jamie needed was a permanent home, a family and a husband who knew how to make her happy.

He had no business thinking he could give her that. He'd made her miserable when he'd been married to her before. She'd hated the long hours, the frequent moves, the sense of never belonging to a place or a community.

His career wasn't even the main issue. Even if he quit TV news for a more settled job, he still had no qualifications for being a good husband or parent, no experience at being part of a loving family. Those were things she needed in a mate, and he didn't know if he had them to give. He didn't think a person could give away something they'd never had.

He'd hurt her before, and he didn't want hurt her again. She'd be better off if he simply got out of her life.

He suddenly realized Todd was standing a short distance away. Dropping Jamie's hands, Stone frowned and motioned him over. "Chuck is supposed to be handling this spot," he told him, naming the head of the promotions department.

Todd's Adam's apple bobbed nervously. "He's out with the flu. He asked me to stand in for him for today's taping."

"This promo is important, Todd." Stone leveled his sternest look at him. "I personally wrote it and I want it to go as planned."

"Of course." Todd gave a nervous smile and hurried away.

Jamie placed a hand on Stone's arm. "Is it really necessary? After all, I'm only going to be on the anchor desk a couple more weeks."

"But the next two weeks are the last half of sweeps," he reminded her. "We've got to do everything we can to drive up the ratings. It's important for the sale of the station."

"Any buyers on the horizon?"

"Two. That's why I'm going to Chicago."

"Stone!" yelled Michael.

Stone looked up to find the boy racing toward him. The next thing he knew, a small pair of arms were tightly wound around his neck and a bubble-gum-scented cheek was pressed against his own.

"Hi, sport." Grinning, Stone swung the child around like a sack of potatoes, relishing the boy's open affection. He'd gotten close to the kid over the past few weeks. It touched something deep inside him to see Michael's face light up at the sight of him.

As the child squealed in delight, Stone swung him upside down, then set him on his feet.

"That was fun!" Michael exclaimed, climbing on Stone's back for a piggyback ride.

Stone hoisted the boy onto his shoulders and glanced at Jamie. The sunlight gleamed on her golden hair and danced across her smiling face, glinting off her impossibly blue eyes. She looked all lit up from inside, like an angel at the top of a Christmas tree.

He gazed at her, trying to memorize the way she looked. He wanted to remember every detail so that he could relive this moment when he was gone.

The thought drained the joy out of him like a pulled bathtub plug.

He set Michael on the ground and deliberately turned his attention to the youngster, forcing a levity into his voice that he suddenly didn't feel. "Are you all set to be a TV star, Michael?"

The boy shook his mop of dark curls.

"Why not? It'll help you find a family."

"But I've already found the family I want." The boy looked earnestly at Stone. "I want you and Jamie."

Oh, jeez. He should have foreseen this. Stone swallowed hard and avoided Jamie's eyes. "Jamie and I aren't a family, Michael."

"You would be if you got married."

"Michael, it's not that easy."

"Why not?" The child persisted. "Don't you love her?"

Stone shifted uneasily and shoved his hands in his pockets, his eyes on the ground. If he admitted his feelings, it would just complicate things further. "There's more to marriage than that," he evaded.

"Like what?"

Stone's palms grew damp. "Well, like...compatibility."

"Aren't you and Jamie 'patible?"

The achingly innocent question hung in the air. Stone's eyes met Jamie's over the youngster's head, and the pain and confusion in her expression hit him like a blow to the stomach.

Oh Lord, he hadn't wanted to hurt her. What had he been thinking?

He'd selfishly soaked up her time and attention like a cactus preparing for a drought, deluding himself that he wouldn't hurt her if he didn't make love to her.

What a fool he was. What a damned, selfish fool.

He pulled his eyes away and drew a deep breath. "People can like each other a whole lot, Michael, but still not be right to marry each other. They need to want the same things out of life, to be able to help make each other's dreams come true. Sometimes that's just not possible, even when two people really care about each other."

Michael's shoulders slumped. "So you and Jamie aren't getting married again?"

Stone's mouth suddenly went dry. He could feel the heat of Jamie's gaze on him, but he couldn't bring himself to look at her. The pain he'd already seen in her face was ripping his heart to shreds. The fine lines of hurt radiating from the corners of her eyes, the disbelieving, wounded expression he'd read in their blue depths, the slight wobble of her chin, would probably haunt him for the rest of his life.

He realized the boy was still waiting for an answer. "Michael, this isn't the time or place for this discussion."

Michael heaved a sigh. "That means no. Grown-ups always talk like that when the answer is no."

Stone still tried to avoid Jamie's eyes, but they drew his like a magnet. He looked away, unable to bear the hurt he'd put there.

Dear God, what had he done? He'd never meant to cause her pain.

But clearly he had, and he knew no way to undo the damage. The kindest thing he could do for her now was simply to leave.

He pulled his hands from his pockets. "I'd better go or I'll miss my plane. I'll see you both in a few days."

He strode rapidly down the trail, feeling lower than the heel of his brown leather loafers, mentally calling himself every name in the book.

Someday Jamie might be able to forgive him for coming back and hurting her again, but Stone doubted he'd ever be able to forgive himself.

Chapter Eleven

"Three minutes," called the director.

Jamie slid the wire of the laveliere mike up the inside of her new coat dress and clipped it to the lapel. The blue fabric reminded her of Stone—but then, so did everything.

She exhaled, her heart as heavy as her sigh. She'd bought the outfit weeks ago because blue was Stone's favorite color, and she'd donned it this morning because he was due back today.

Not that he'd notice, she thought bleakly. Not that it would make any difference if he did.

He'd been gone an entire week, and he hadn't called her once. He hadn't sent a fax, a postcard or an E-mail message. He hadn't made any attempt to contact her at all ever since he'd dropped the news that he didn't intend to marry her again.

The thought brought a lump to her throat. She straightened the stack of papers in front of her, carefully aligning the edges, and tried to bring a sense of order to her thoughts, as well.

It was as if the previous weeks hadn't happened—seeing him every day, having dinner with him every night, talking with him on the phone every evening before she went to bed. It was as if he'd never returned at all, as if it had all been a figment of her imagination.

Because here she was, back in the same lonely, loveless void where she'd existed ever since their divorce.

She'd been deluding herself about him, seeing only what she'd wanted to see, she thought glumly. She'd read too much into the physical attraction they still had for each other, and she'd discounted the fact he hadn't told her he loved her or talked about the future.

She'd been as blind and foolish as a lovesick schoolgirl. She'd given up everything for him. Her secrets, her heart…oh, mercy, even her home. She'd been so eager to show him that she loved him she'd never even questioned the depth of his feelings for her.

A cloud of despair settled over her, deepening the dense, gray fog that seemed to be smothering her life. How could she have been so wrong? When he'd told her that day in the park that he wanted to start over with her, she'd been sure he'd meant marriage.

Had something happened to change his mind? If so, what could it have been? Had she done something wrong?

She'd turned the questions over and over in her mind, and finally she'd drawn the conclusion that it really didn't matter. The only thing that mattered was that he didn't want to remarry her. And if she hadn't gotten the message when he said as much to Michael, his failure to call her even once over the past week should have conveyed it loud and clear.

He didn't love her enough to try again.

Jamie stared sightlessly at the papers in her hand. She'd thought she could never hurt worse than she had when they'd ended their marriage.

But she'd been wrong. Because now she knew she'd never gotten over Stone in the first place, and the realization left her without hope for the future. Now she knew she was destined to forever love a man who wouldn't or couldn't love her back.

"One minute," boomed the director.

Jamie sighed. She needed to pull herself together for the next thirty minutes. Michael's story aired today and she had to do her best to help him find a home. There'd be plenty of time later to think about Stone and how she was going to live without him. A whole lifetime, in fact.

Drawing a deep breath, she straightened her back and put the earpiece in place.

"Hey, Jamie, that new promo about you is going to air right before the intro," the director said in her ear. "Have you seen it yet?"

Shaking her head, she turned to watch the monitor as a close-up of her face filled the screen. The picture changed to a montage of shots of her seated at the anchor desk as the background music swelled.

"There's something special about Jamie Erickson, the newest member of the KZZZ news team," intoned the silken voice of the announcer. "You can see it in her smile. You can see it in the way she cares about the news and the people it affects."

Clips of Jamie with various children flashed across the screen with the words "A Home of My Own" superimposed underneath. Footage of Jamie and Michael at the riding stable followed.

"Jamie understands adversity because she lives with it herself. Every time she sits behind this desk—" the screen filled with a dramatic zoom-in shot of the empty anchor desk "—she fights a battle not to stutter. Despite a crippling speech impediment, Jamie puts herself on the line every day to bring you the latest news about your community.

"Jamie Erickson and channel three—going the extra mile to bring you news you can use."

The station's "News You Can Use" logo filled the screen as the music crescendoed to a close.

Jamie stared blankly at the monitor, her blood turning to ice water in her veins, and tried to absorb what she'd just seen.

She felt exposed, as though her new dress were made of clear plastic wrap. She felt mortified.

And betrayed. Completely, utterly betrayed.

By whom? It made no sense.

It made no sense, she thought repeatedly, the thought replaying in her mind like a dubbed tape. How could this have happened? Stone had written the script himself.

Stone. The thought hit her like a sledgehammer, but she rejected it as quickly as it formed.

No. He might not love her, but he would never betray her.

Todd. It was Todd, and he wanted her to think Stone was responsible.

The thought allowed her to draw a breath, but another, more immediate worry kept the air from quite reaching her lungs.

The viewers know I have a speech impediment. Everyone is waiting for me to stutter.

The news introduction was nearly over. Panic squeezed her like a set of cold, clammy tentacles, and her throat tensed until it was impossible to breathe, much less speak.

"You okay, doll? Here we go." Harold's face crinkled into a worried frown as he pulled down his arm to signal she was on the air.

Jamie stared at the red light at the top of the camera and opened her mouth, but nothing came out.

"You're on, Jamie," the producer said in her ear.

She stared blindly ahead, unable to move, her body as numb as her heart, paralyzed with pain and terror.

"Come on! Come on!" the director hissed.

Concentrate, she told herself, but her thoughts were as loose and disconnected as a box of jigsaw puzzle pieces. What was it she had told Michael just a week ago? She couldn't remember, but the very thought of Michael touched a surviving nerve.

His story was due to air today. He was watching.

The thought gave her a point of focus, cutting through her fear like a beam of light shining through a fog. She

aimed toward it, struggling against the panic like a swim-
mer against a current.

He was watching, and she couldn't let him down. She
couldn't let him see her immobilized by her speech impediment. He might never believe he could overcome his own
disability if she failed to conquer hers now.

She took a deep breath, concentrated all her thoughts on
the child and gave it all she had. "G-g-g-g-g-good aftern-
n-n-noon," she croaked.

The director shouted something in her IFB. She needed
to focus, and she couldn't do it while he was yammering
in her ear. She yanked out the earpiece.

"I'm J-J-J-J-Jamie Erickson, and th-th-this is the n-noon
news." She picked up the sheet of paper in front of her
and concentrated on the meaning behind the words, trying
to lose herself in the story. After the first few words, her
stuttering abated.

By the time Harold's camera light blinked off at the end
of the newscast, she was wringing wet.

She might have stuttered on the air, but she'd made it
through the newscast. It was her personal nightmare, her
own worst-case scenario, and she'd lived through it. The
world had not come to an end, the walls had not fallen
around her.

The fear clutching her chest loosened its grip, and she
instinctively knew it would never hold her in its clutches
that tightly again.

She was free. Maybe not of the stuttering, but of the
terror that had held her captive. The secret was out. The
whole world now knew she stuttered, and with the secrecy
dissolved, so was the fear. She drew a deep breath and felt
a sweet surge of freedom fill her chest, then flow through
her veins like oxygen.

She detached the mike and rose from her chair, her
thoughts on Michael. Oh, dear. He probably wouldn't see
the victory; he would only see that she'd stuttered on the
air.

She bit the inside of her lip. She didn't want him to lose

confidence in his ability to conquer his problem. She couldn't let him give in to the fear, couldn't let it limit his choices in life.

"You okay?" Harold asked worriedly.

"I'm fine," she said, stepping off the set, her mouth set in a determined line. "And I'm going to the children's home to make sure Michael knows he will be, too."

When Stone arrived in the newsroom twenty minutes later, he could have sworn the reception he got was less than warm. In fact, it seemed downright chilly.

The news secretary's response to his question about Jamie's whereabouts was short and snippy, the assignment editor averted his face the moment he saw him, and the reporters standing around the water cooler cast silent glares in his direction.

He strode toward a familiar figure by the coffeepot. "Hello, Harold."

The large man mounted a scowl and buried his face in a coffee mug. "Harrumph."

Something was up, all right, and Stone intended to find out what it was. He folded his arms across his chest. "All right, Harold. What's going on around here?"

Harold set down the cup hard enough to slosh coffee over the sides. "That was a rotten stunt you pulled on Jamie."

"What are you talking about?"

Harold lifted a furry brow and gave him a look that could have scorched asbestos. "You know what I'm talkin' about. That damned promotion tellin' the world she stutters and how she goes on the air afraid it'll happen at any time."

Stone stared at Harold. "The promotion said *what?*"

"You heard me."

"The spot I wrote and ordered to be produced said no such thing." His words were clipped and hard, his voice edged with fury. It only hinted at the turbulence brewing inside him. His muscles tensed and his hands balled into fists. "Tell me what happened."

"Well, it aired right before today's noon news. It broadsided Jamie—sent her into a tailspin. She couldn't talk at first, but she pulled out of it and finished the newscast."

Stone's fingers curled so tightly his short, clipped nails bit into his palms.

"The phones were ringing off the wall," Harold continued. "Half the people called because they think she hung the moon. The other half think the station is lower than a snake's wanky tank for exploiting her like that."

Evidently the staff thought the same thing, Stone reflected grimly. And judging from the glares he was receiving, they thought he was responsible.

Oh Lord. Did Jamie think so, too? The thought hit him hard, like a solid fist in the gut.

"Where is she?"

"She went to the children's home. She was worried about how Michael might react."

That was so like her, Stone thought, his heart a heavy, aching weight in his chest. She'd just lived through the most humiliating moment of her life, but her thoughts were focused on someone else.

Her heart was so kind, so loving. And when she gave it to someone, she gave it unconditionally—through thick and thin, through good and bad...

For better or for worse.

The thought stopped him cold, and his throat grew so tight he could barely breathe.

Oh God, he was an even bigger fool than he'd thought he was. Why hadn't he seen it earlier?

It wasn't the say-so of some two-bit, would-be minister at a fly-by-night wedding chapel that had married them. A flimsy piece of paper signed by some black-robed judge hadn't managed to unmarry them, either.

They'd been married in the eyes of God when they'd promised to love each other for better or worse, for richer or poorer, in sickness or in health, till death did they part.

He'd meant those vows when he'd spoken them, and he knew Jamie had, too.

In his heart of hearts, she was still his wife. If Jamie felt anything about him like he felt about her, she'd never be happy without him.

Who the hell was he to determine if she'd be better off without him? That was for her to decide.

Hope flooded his veins, along with a rush of adrenaline. If she would take him back, he'd consider himself the luckiest damn fool on the face of the earth. And he'd spend the rest of his life trying to be the kind of man she deserved.

Stone looked at Harold. "I want to see the tape of the newscast. Then I want to see Todd."

Comprehension streaked across Harold's face like dawn's early light. "You mean that sorry piece of work did this to Jamie? Why, that lousy, no-good, rotten..."

Stone lifted his hand. "Save it for later, Harold, and just bring me the tape. I'm in a hurry to get this thing settled so I can go settle a more important matter with Jamie."

Chapter Twelve

"I dunno," Michael said dubiously. "I still think I would have run away."

Jamie added another wooden block to the tower she and the boy were building on the floor of the playroom at the children's home. "If I'd run away, your story might not have made air. And it was important to me to try to find you a home."

"But didn't you feel bad?"

Jamie smiled into his earnest hazel eyes. "Yes. But I would have felt worse if I'd run away. By staying, I got the stuttering under control and I got to finish what I started."

"Weren't you scared?"

Jamie nodded. "Sure I was. But I didn't want the fear to win. By not quitting, I won. And the fear won't ever be that strong again, because now I know I can beat it."

"That's what's known as courage," said a deep male voice from the doorway.

"Stone!" Michael yelled, jumping to his feet.

Jamie clutched a hand to her chest as the boy hurled

himself at Stone like a cannonball. Her heart pounding, she watched Stone hug the boy, then set him on the floor.

"Michael, I need to talk to Jamie alone. Why don't you go play outside with the other kids, and we'll come get you in a few minutes."

"Then can we go for ice cream?" Michael asked.

"You bet."

Michael darted from the room, and she found herself suddenly alone with Stone. She stared up at him, panic-stricken and frozen, not knowing what to do or what to say, now that everything had changed between them.

No, that wasn't right; nothing had changed, nothing concrete. Just her perception of things—of their relationship, of what they meant to each other, of their future.

Nothing, that was, except her whole world. It had crumbled when he'd as much as said he didn't intend to marry her again. She rose on shaky legs, straightened her dress and pulled herself to her full height. Folding her arms protectively over her chest, she strove to project some semblance of normalcy. "When did you get back?"

"An hour ago. I went straight to the station from the airport. Jamie, I heard what happened on the newscast." He stepped toward her and placed his hands on her upper arms, the space between his brows creased with concern. "I'm so sorry. I hope..." His brown eyes met hers, and the emotion she saw there nearly shattered her thin shell of composure. How could he look like this, so warm and concerned and caring, and plan to just walk away from her? "I hope you know I didn't write it like that."

The worry in his eyes cut right through her, destroying the protective barricade she'd tried to erect around her heart. Did he really think she'd blame him? No matter how badly he'd hurt her, she couldn't bear the thought of hurting him back. And nothing would wound him as deeply as having his integrity doubted. For too much of his life, his integrity was all that he'd had.

"No, I knew it wasn't you," she reassured him softly. "It was Todd, wasn't it?"

Stone nodded, his mouth grim. "He admitted it when I confronted him." No point in telling her he'd backed Todd against a wall and threatened to mop the room with him unless he told the truth. "He thought that if you stuttered on the air, you'd quit and he'd get his old job back. He broke down and cried—admitted he has a drinking problem, said it's messed up his thinking." Stone raked a hand through his hair. "He's agreed to go to treatment. When he comes back, he'll be on probation. The slightest infraction and he's out the door."

"I've always felt sorry for Todd," Jamie murmured. "I've always thought he was in the grip of something bigger than he was, something he couldn't control. It was kind of you to talk Mr. Milton into not firing him."

Stone thought her eyes held more sympathy than Todd deserved. "Actually, it's not Mr. Milton's decision anymore," he replied.

Jamie's eyebrows rose. "You mean the station's been sold?"

Stone nodded. "And Mr. Milton's finally getting to retire like he wanted. The new owner is going to act as general manager."

"Is everyone's job safe?"

Stone nodded. "That was one of the stipulations in the contract. Lucky for Todd, all the staff has job security for at least the next six months."

"Who's the new owner?"

Stone paused for a heartbeat, then grinned. "I am."

Jamie stared at him, her eyes wide, her lips parted. "You?"

"Yep." He couldn't keep the proud grin off his face. "I'm the new owner, and I'm sticking around."

Jamie's heart thundered in her chest as her emotions swung between joy and despair. He was staying! But, oh, mercy, that meant seeing him every day, working beside him, knowing he didn't love her as she loved him.

When she finally found her voice, it came out wobbly and weak. "This is the career change you mentioned?"

Stone nodded. "But until the very last minute, it looked like it wasn't going to work. Another company nearly out-bid me."

"Why on earth didn't you tell me?"

He shrugged his massive shoulders. "I wanted to be sure I could work it out."

"But how? Why?"

"I put together a group of financial backers, primarily former clients. Since I'm the consultant, I had to make sure the station would do well in the ratings, so it wouldn't look like I was sabotaging things to get the cost down. That's why I pressed so hard to keep you on the air. But enough about that." He gave a slow grin. "I'd rather address the 'why' part of your question."

He took a step toward her, picked up a lock of her hair and twirled it around a finger. "I figured if I owned a station, I could stay in one place and hire other people to work the late shifts and weekends. I can't promise I won't still put in some late hours, but work won't be my life." His dark eyes gleamed in the sunlight filtering through the window. "You will. That is, if you'll have me back."

Her pulse raced so hard she could hear the blood pounding in her ears. Was he asking what she thought he was asking? She didn't dare make any more assumptions.

He stepped closer until she could smell his faint, familiar scent.

"When I got back here and discovered what had happened—Jamie, I was beside myself." His hands moved to her arms. "I saw the tape of the newscast. Honey, what you did today was the bravest thing I've ever seen."

Jamie gazed up at him, her heart tripping so erratically that she could barely follow his words.

"I decided then and there that if you can face your worst fears, then I can face mine, too." His gaze was blunt and open, and his eyes held a naked vulnerability she'd never seen before. "I'm scared to death of hurting you again, Jamie. I'm scared of letting you down, of not being what you need. But, Jamie, I want to try. More than anything I've ever wanted, I want to try."

His dark eyes scanning hers, he cupped a hand under her chin. "I've never stopped loving you, Jamie. Will you marry me again?"

"Oh, Stone..." Her voice cracked, and she couldn't speak. All she could do was look up, touch his face and let him read the answer in her eyes as she gave a barely perceptible nod of her head.

His eyes full of emotion, he swept her to him and lowered his lips to hers.

Long moments and many whispered endearments later, he pulled back and gazed down at her. "Now that I own the station, I get to make the rules. And the first one is you're hereby released from your contract. You don't have to go back on the air at all if you don't want to."

If her heart was soaring before, it skyrocketed now. She was where she'd always wanted to be—in his arms, in his heart, at the top of his priority list. She gazed up at him, her heart full and overflowing, her eyes in the same condition, feeling loved as she'd never felt loved before. With all her heart she longed to make him feel loved in return.

She gave him a tremulous smile. "Wait just a minute there, Johnson. Didn't you just say you're the owner of the station now?"

"Yes." His brow quirked in that familiar I-know-you're-up-to-something look.

"And didn't you just pay top dollar for it, based on a projection we'd do well in the sweeps?"

"Yes," he said slowly.

Her smile brightened until it gleamed like a klieg light. In all of his life, he'd never seen anything lovelier.

"Then by golly, Stone, we'll need to get top dollar in ad revenue, won't we? If we're going to run a television station, we darn well better make a profit at it, don't you think?"

He loved the way that little word sounded on her lips—

we. He tried to pretend to be weighing her question, but he was grinning so hard his face hurt. "I suppose we should."

"Then I need to stay on at the anchor desk," she said decisively. "At least for the time being. Later on, when the newsroom is squared away, you can plan a time slot for a local children's program. I know a producer who'll do a great job with the right motivation."

"I can't wait to provide that motivation." His hand feathered down her cheek. Her skin felt as soft as the down of a dove. "Honey, do you have any idea how much I love you?"

She gave him a mischievous grin as she fitted herself against him. "I have a concept."

He laughed, his heart somersaulting with joy. He looked in her eyes and basked in what he saw there.

"I love you, Stone," she murmured. "And I want to be your wife. In every way."

Oh, how he'd longed to hear those words! His throat grew thick and tight with emotion, and his voice was husky when he spoke. "And I can't wait to be your husband." His fingers tightened on her back. "Let's get married as soon as possible."

She nodded. "But first we've got to find a place to live."

Stone's eyebrows flew up in surprise. "What do you mean?"

"I sold my house."

He stared at her. She didn't look like she was kidding. "You what?"

"Well, I had no way of knowing the career changes you were talking about would keep you in Fairfield. And I wasn't going to let you leave without me. Not again."

He knew how much that house meant to her. A lump the size of Texas formed in his throat. She'd been ready and willing to give up her lifelong dream in order to be with him. He shook his head in amazement. He didn't know how he'd managed to win the heart of a woman this wonderful, but he was determined to do everything in his power to make sure he kept her.

She gave him a slightly crooked smile. Her eyes were the color of a clear sky. "It was just a house." She placed her cool palm against his cheek. "Home is where the heart is. And mine will always be with you."

Stone's heart was so full of love it felt as though it would burst from his chest. He gathered her closer against him.

"Welcome home, honey," he murmured, his voice thick and raw with emotion.

Her arms curled around him. He could feel her fingers threading through the back of his hair.

"Welcome home," she whispered.

Epilogue

"This cake is delicious!" Harold mumbled as he shoveled another forkful of white frosting into his mouth.

A warm breeze caught the rim of Grams's wide-brimmed straw hat, and she clamped a hand on top to hold it in place, juggling her plate of cake in the other. "Glad you like it. It's a recipe from the 'Happy Homemaker' show. I didn't have time to bake it myself, but I gave the recipe to the caterer." Grams's cheeks formed two bright apples as she smiled. "My travel schedule keeps me pretty busy, now that I'm a working gal."

Jamie grinned up at Stone as they strolled past. "Grams is so proud to be taking over your television consulting business."

Stone's eyes danced as he glanced down at her. "She's a natural. I've never met anyone with more talent for recognizing what the public really wants. Everyone loves her offbeat suggestions."

"I believe Grams prefers the term *innovative*."

Stone grinned. "Whatever you call them, the stations are thrilled with the results. And I'm thrilled I get to stay home with my wife."

Stone tightened his grip on Jamie's waist as they stopped beneath the arched rose trellis in Grams's backyard, watching their guests mill about the linen-draped tables. His gaze drifted down and locked on her face. "Have I told you how beautiful you look today?"

Jamie smiled up at her handsome husband, her white wedding dress billowing around her. "Only about a dozen times."

"Hmm. Some things bear repeating." His eyes held a look of love and pride warmer than the afternoon sun.

"There's one thing I'm awfully glad we repeated—our wedding vows. And I'm glad we were married in a church," Jamie said softly.

"Me, too." Stone squeezed her waist and angled a glance down at her. "I always wanted to see you in a dress like that. I cheated you out of a white gown and all the trimmings the last time we got married."

"I never minded."

"Well, now we'll have a proper set of wedding pictures to show our children. Besides, a formal wedding gave us a great excuse for a party." He grinned, showing his white, straight teeth. "Marriage brings lots of reasons to celebrate. Let's see...the next occasion will be a housewarming celebration when the builders clear out of that barn we're building."

Jamie laughed. "It's not a barn. It's a farmhouse."

His dimple flashed roguishly. "I don't care if it's a chicken coop, as long as it makes you happy—and has a double bed."

A sweet rush of anticipation swept through her as she thought of the night ahead. There would be time later, when they were alone, to tell him all the warm, sultry emotions he kindled in her when he looked at her like that.

The squeal of a child's laughter drew their attention across the lawn. Michael barreled toward them like a small torpedo, and Stone laughed as he scooped the boy up in his arms.

"I was a good ring bearer, wasn't I?" Michael beamed.

"You were terrific," Stone told him.

"Now that you're married, can I call you Mom and Dad?"

Stone gazed over the boy's curly head at Jamie, and the tenderness in his expression brought tears to her eyes. He gave the boy a squeeze, and when he spoke, his voice was husky with emotion. "You bet, son."

"I can't wait to move in with you guys!" he said.

"Just as soon as we get back from our honeymoon," Jamie promised.

Mrs. Mathis came up and led Michael off to get some wedding cake.

Stone put his arm around Jamie and watched the small boy skip across the lawn. "I'm glad Mrs. Mathis arranged for us to get custody of him so quickly."

Jamie smiled in agreement. "Me, too. Making us foster parents until the adoption is finalized was a great idea."

"We'll need to have another party in a few months to celebrate signing the official papers," Stone said. "And then we'll need to have christening parties for all those other children we're going to have." His eyes gleamed a private message. "We should probably get started on that project right away."

"Perhaps we should wait until the honeymoon," she said with a wry smile.

"If you insist." Their eyes locked, attraction crackling between them. His lips descended to softly brush hers, the kiss as tender as a caress. They drew back and looked at each other, their gaze a promise of things to come.

"Have I told you how beautiful you are?" he asked.

"There you go, repeating yourself again," Jamie teased.

"Can I help it if I'm completely, irretrievably besotted with my wife?"

Jamie stretched her arms around his neck, snuggling against him. The fit was like a hand in a glove, a key in a lock, a door in a doorjamb. It was solid and warm and welcoming, safe and cozy, yet indescribably thrilling.

It was where she belonged, where she wanted to stay.

It was everything she'd ever wanted a home to be.

"I love you, Stone," she whispered.

"And I love you," he rasped against her hair.

"You can repeat that just as often as you like," she murmured as she stood on tiptoe to meet his kiss. "Preferably daily. For the rest of our lives."

* * * * *

If you enjoyed HUSBAND AND WIFE...AGAIN, be sure to pick up Robin's next novel, HAVE HONEYMOON, NEED HUSBAND, coming July 1997 from Silhouette Romance.

Silhouette ROMANCE™

cordially invites you to the unplanned nuptials
of three unsuspecting hunks and their

SURPRISE
BRIDES

Look for the following specially packaged titles:

March 1997: MISSING: ONE BRIDE by Alice Sharpe, #1212
April 1997: LOOK-ALIKE BRIDE by Laura Anthony, #1220
May 1997: THE SECRET GROOM by Myrna Mackenzie, #1225

Don't miss **Surprise Brides**, an irresistible trio of books about love
and marriage by three talented authors! Found only in—

Silhouette ROMANCE™

SR-BRIDE

Take 4 bestselling love stories FREE

Plus get a FREE surprise gift!

Special Limited-time Offer

Mail to Silhouette Reader Service™

3010 Walden Avenue
P.O. Box 1867
Buffalo, N.Y. 14240-1867

YES! Please send me 4 free Silhouette Romance™ novels and my free surprise gift. Then send me 6 brand-new novels every month, which I will receive months before they appear in bookstores. Bill me at the low price of $2.67 each plus 25¢ delivery and applicable sales tax, if any.* That's the complete price and a savings of over 10% off the cover prices—quite a bargain! I understand that accepting the books and gift places me under no obligation ever to buy any books. I can always return a shipment and cancel at any time. Even if I never buy another book from Silhouette, the 4 free books and the surprise gift are mine to keep forever.

215 BPA A3UT

Name	(PLEASE PRINT)	
Address	Apt. No.	
City	State	Zip

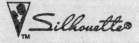

As seen on TV!
Free Gift Offer

With a Free Gift proof-of-purchase from any Silhouette® book,
you can receive a beautiful cubic zirconia pendant.

This gorgeous marquise-shaped stone is a genuine cubic
zirconia—accented by an 18" gold tone necklace.

(Approximate retail value $19.95)

Send for yours today...
compliments of 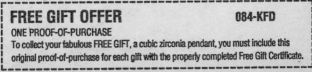 *Silhouette*®

To receive your free gift, a cubic zirconia pendant, send us one original proof-of-purchase, photocopies not accepted, from the back of any Silhouette Romance™, Silhouette Desire®, Silhouette Special Edition®, Silhouette Intimate Moments® or Silhouette Yours Truly™ title available in February, March and April at your favorite retail outlet, together with the Free Gift Certificate, plus a check or money order for $1.65 U.S./$2.15 CAN. (do not send cash) to cover postage and handling, payable to Silhouette Free Gift Offer. We will send you the specified gift. Allow 6 to 8 weeks for delivery. Offer good until April 30, 1997 or while quantities last. Offer valid in the U.S. and Canada only.

Free Gift Certificate

Name: _____

Address: _____

City: _____ State/Province: _____ Zip/Postal Code: _____

Mail this certificate, one proof-of-purchase and a check or money order for postage and handling to: SILHOUETTE FREE GIFT OFFER 1997. In the U.S.: 3010 Walden Avenue, P.O. Box 9077, Buffalo NY 14269-9077. In Canada: P.O. Box 613, Fort Erie, Ontario L2Z 5X3.

FREE GIFT OFFER   084-KFD
ONE PROOF-OF-PURCHASE
To collect your fabulous FREE GIFT, a cubic zirconia pendant, you must include this
original proof-of-purchase for each gift with the properly completed Free Gift Certificate.

084-KFD

IN CELEBRATION OF MOTHER'S DAY, JOIN
SILHOUETTE THIS MAY AS WE BRING YOU

a funny thing
HAPPENED ON THE WAY TO THE
Delivery Room

THESE THREE STORIES, CELEBRATING THE
LIGHTER SIDE OF MOTHERHOOD, ARE
WRITTEN BY YOUR FAVORITE AUTHORS:

KASEY MICHAELS
KATHLEEN EAGLE
EMILIE RICHARDS

When three couples make the trip to the delivery
room, they get more than their own bundles of
joy…they get the promise of love!

Available this May,
wherever Silhouette books are sold.

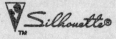

You're About to Become a

Privileged Woman

Reap the rewards of fabulous free gifts and benefits with proofs-of-purchase from Silhouette and Harlequin books

Pages & Privileges™

It's our way of thanking you for buying our books at your favorite retail stores.

PROOF OF PURCHASE

SR-PP23

Offer expires March 31, 1997

Pages & Privileges ™

Harlequin and Silhouette— the most privileged readers in the world!

For more information about Harlequin and Silhouette's PAGES & PRIVILEGES program call the Pages & Privileges Benefits Desk: 1-503-794-2499

Silhouette®

SR-PP23